P9-DCO-614

THE DARKDEEP

ALLY CONDIE
BRENDAN REICHS

BLOOMSBURY
CHILDREN'S BOOKS
NEW YORK LONDON OXFORD NEW DELHI SYDNEY

BLOOMSBURY CHILDREN'S BOOKS
Bloomsbury Publishing Inc., part of Bloomsbury Publishing Plc
1385 Broadway, New York, NY 10018

BLOOMSBURY, BLOOMSBURY CHILDREN'S BOOKS, and the Diana logo
are trademarks of Bloomsbury Publishing Plc

First published in the United States of America in October 2018
by Bloomsbury Children's Books

Text copyright © 2018 by Allyson Braithwaite Condie and Brendan C. Reichs
Illustrations copyright © 2018 by Antonio Javier Caparo

All rights reserved. No part of this publication may be reproduced or
transmitted in any form or by any means, electronic or mechanical, including
photocopying, recording, or any information storage or retrieval system, without
prior permission in writing from the publisher.

Bloomsbury books may be purchased for business or promotional use.
For information on bulk purchases please contact Macmillan Corporate and
Premium Sales Department at specialmarkets@macmillan.com

Library of Congress Cataloging-in-Publication Data
Names: Condie, Allyson Braithwaite, author. | Reichs, Brendan, author.
Title: The Darkdeep / by Ally Condie and Brendan Reichs.
Description: New York : Bloomsbury, 2018.
Summary: Middle-schoolers Nico, Tyler, Emma, and Opal discover a hidden island in a
forbidden cove that appears uninhabited, but something ancient has awakened knowing
their wishes, dreams, and darkest secrets.
Identifiers: LCCN 2018024232 (print) | LCCN 2018030596 (e-book)
ISBN 978-1-5476-0046-5 (hardcover) • ISBN 978-1-5476-0047-2 (e-book)
Subjects: | CYAC: Supernatural—Fiction. | Houseboats—Fiction. | Islands—Fiction. |
Friendship—Fiction. | Northwest, Pacific—Fiction. | Horror stories.
Classification: LCC PZ7.C7586 Dar 2018 (print) | LCC PZ7.C7586 (e-book) |
DDC[Fic]—dc23
LC record available at https://lccn.loc.gov/2018024232

ISBN 978-1-5476-0215-5 (special edition)

Book design by Jeanette Levy
Typeset by Westchester Publishing Services
Printed and bound in the U.S.A. by Berryville Graphics Inc., Berryville, Virginia
2 4 6 8 10 9 7 5 3 1

All papers used by Bloomsbury Publishing Plc are natural, recyclable products
made from wood grown in well-managed forests. The manufacturing processes
conform to the environmental regulations of the country of origin.

To find out more about our authors and books visit
www.bloomsbury.com and sign up for our newsletters.

For Jodi,
with gratitude, admiration,
and a little bit of fear

PART ONE

TIMBERS

1

NICO

The ground leaped up to smack Nico in the face.

Air exploded from his lungs as he tumbled down a steep slope. The drone barely missed him, buzzing the grass before shooting out over a cliff choked by dark, swirling mists.

Nearly killed by my own quadcopter. Jeez.

Nico heard pounding feet. A wide-eyed Tyler Watson appeared at the top of the rise, sunglasses wedged into his old-school box haircut. A moment later Emma Fairington appeared beside him with the remote in her hands.

"Sorry, sorry!" Tyler gripped his head. "I think the controller jammed or something!"

"Nothing jammed," Emma snapped. "You forgot how the switches work. Press *down* to go up, genius."

"Who makes controls like that?" Tyler shot back.

A moment later the drone zoomed out of the fog, arcing high above the cloudy Pacific Northwest coastline. Nico grunted in relief, pushing chestnut-brown hair out of his eyes. "Good flying, Emma. I owe you the ice cream of your choice."

Emma nodded in full agreement. "Rocky Road. Duh."

"See? Everything's fine." Tyler heaved a sigh, then held up a finger. "Now, the *important* thing is that Nico's drone is safe. So let's not waste time figuring out who almost killed who with what."

"Right." Nico rolled his eyes.

"Could've been anybody, really." Tyler was short and skinny, with dark skin and an infectious smile. He peered down at Nico, who was sprawled only a body-length short of a *loooong* drop over the same fog-shrouded cliff. Now that he knew his friend was okay, Tyler could barely contain his laughter. "You, uh . . . you all right there, Nico? That looked painful."

Nico felt lucky to be in one piece. He liked to play things cool, but there was nothing cool about throwing yourself down a hill to avoid a streaking thirty-pound drone. Not with his dad upriver at a forestry station, and his brother away at college. Twelve was considered old enough to take care of yourself in the Holland family, but not if you ended up in the hospital.

"I'm great." Nico spat grass from his teeth. "But next time, try not to kill me with my own invention."

"*Your* invention?" Tyler snorted as he tromped down to lend Nico a hand. "You'd never have gotten it out of the box

4

without us." His laughter escaped, and Nico joined in. That's just how it was with Tyler.

"It was my fault, too," Emma admitted as the boys walked uphill to join her. "I was giving Ty flight directions. We were trying to re-create that scene in *Rogue One* where X-wings attack the beach." Her blue eyes twinkled as she mimicked a dive-bombing action with her hands. Emma was always talking about movies, both her sci-fi favorites and the ones she meant to film someday. Nico usually found it entertaining, when he wasn't in the line of fire.

"We got *epic* footage," Tyler said. "Dude, your face as you ran for your life? Priceless."

"It's really great!" Emma waved her phone. "Wanna watch yourself flip over in slo-mo?"

"Pass." Nico blinked to clear his head. "I'm seeing three phones right now."

Emma's face fell, but Nico bumped her shoulder with his to show he was kidding. She glanced into the fog behind them and shivered. "Let's check the drone. Maybe we should fly it somewhere else."

Tyler nodded quickly. "Anyplace away from this nightmare factory is fine by me."

Nico understood. No one liked being this close to Still Cove. They jogged back across the grass to inspect the quadcopter.

They'd biked to this remote field—five miles northeast of Timbers, beyond even the old fort at Razor Point—because it was the flattest stretch along this area of Washington shore-line, and the winds were milder there than anywhere else. Plus, it bordered no-man's-land, which meant they'd be alone.

Nico glanced back at the mist. Every kid in Timbers had grown up on horror stories about Still Cove, a dead-end back-water ringed by cliffs and covered by perpetual fog. With sheer walls, jagged rocks, and odd currents, the inlet was con-sidered too dangerous for boats. And then there were the whispers about the Beast.

Those kept people away for sure. Tourists might chuckle about Skagit Sound's legendary sea monster, but the locals didn't. Too many boats had gone missing.

Yet Nico had wanted calm skies to test his quadcopter. He'd spent four weeks and six hundred bucks building it. That was all his money in the world. He jumped as Emma put a hand on his shoulder. She didn't notice, staring grimly into the mists. "I'll never get used to this place," she said quietly.

To their right, the air above Skagit Sound was cloudy but normal. Gentle waves lapped a beach far below the bluffs. But dead ahead, Still Cove was living up to its name—it was roofed cliff to cliff by a thick carpet of fog, like it occupied a sepa-rate ecosystem.

Emma shivered. "Do you really think the Beast lives down there?"

"Don't talk about it," Tyler squawked, his good humor evaporating. "I'm trying not to think about how dumb we are for coming this close. It's like ringing a dinner bell."

Nico snorted. "Dude, come on. There's no such thing as a sea monster."

"That's what people who get eaten by sea monsters say." Tyler slapped down his shades. "Y'all heard what happened to *The Merry Trawler*, right? My sister said that boat drifted into the marina with bite marks *a yard wide*."

Tyler's dad was the town harbormaster. His mom was the head of the Lighthouse Preservation Society, and his older sister, Gabrielle, worked on fishing charters during the summer. Overall, the Watsons knew more about the Sound than any other family in Timbers, but Tyler hated the ocean.

"Your sister knows you'll believe anything she says," Nico teased, but he couldn't help peeking at the mist. *You really can't see through it.* "Let's get the quad airborne again," he said, shaking off a chill. "I want to try some inversions, maybe test its range."

"Stop using words you don't understand," Tyler sniped, and they both laughed.

An owl fluttered up over the cliff, landing with a screech and staring death at the drone. Emma clasped her hands together as the bird ruffled its feathers. "Oh, he's *mad*. Is that one of the owls all the fuss is about?"

Nico's grin died. He kicked a pebble. "I dunno. Maybe."

Emma winced. "Sorry, Nico. I forgot."

A year ago, Nico's father had filed a complaint alleging that logging activities of the Nantes Timber Company—the town's biggest employer—were threatening the nesting grounds for a species of endangered spotted owls. The court agreed and declared thousands of acres off-limits. The company's owner, Sylvain Nantes, had chosen to lay off dozens of workers as a result.

The firings hurt the entire town. Nico and his dad now got dirty looks everywhere they went. Warren Holland was impervious to the negativity, believing firmly in his job with the park service. Nico, however, felt every single glare.

"Well, I think they're beautiful," Emma said as the owl flew away. "They *should* be protected." Nico nodded but remained silent.

"Let's see how the drone is holding up," Tyler said to change the subject. They were inspecting its undercarriage when a new sound broke the silence—a rumbling purr Nico felt deep in his stomach. He thought he recognized the noise, and it wasn't good news. A beat later, two blurs crested the rise across the field.

Four-wheelers. Shiny chrome ones. Nico's heart sank into his shoes.

Only a few kids in Timbers had their own ATVs.

The taller driver straightened in his seat and pointed. Engines roared as the four-wheelers raced directly toward Nico and his friends. They began circling, the drivers laughing and gesturing as they rolled to a halt. The tall one removed his helmet, revealing a sweaty tangle of glossy black hair. Dark eyes regarded them.

Logan Nantes. Nico ran a hand over his face.

"Look at this!" Logan called out. "The weirdos have a model airplane."

Carson Brandt laughed, removing a helmet painted like a skull. He vaulted off the other ATV, farm-boy freckles crinkling on his sunburned nose. Parker Masterson dismounted behind him, flashing a cruel sneer.

"It's not a *plane*." Tyler took off his sunglasses, his eyes somehow narrowing and growing sullen at the same time. "It's a Phantom 3 quadcopter. A *drone*, man. We built it."

"Nobody cares," Carson fired back. Tyler's head dropped.

Nico swallowed, scanning the newcomers for a friendly face. He found none.

Although, to be fair, Opal Walsh didn't look like she wanted to be there. She dismounted behind Logan and crossed her arms, her long black braid draping over one shoulder. Opal wore the expression of someone being forced to watch a show they didn't like.

Their eyes met, and something moved behind Opal's. A flicker of . . . unease? Sympathy? Embarrassment? It vanished as quickly as it came. She glanced away, making it clear Nico shouldn't expect any help from her.

I shared my pudding cups with you in kindergarten, you dumb jerk. But Nico didn't have time to glare at his former friend. Logan was right in front of him.

"Hey, Mr. Animal Planet," Logan said, drawing laughter

from Carson and Parker. Opal scuffed her sneaker in the dirt. Nico wondered what she was doing out with those meat-heads, but that was a question for later. He had to focus on the predator in front of him.

Don't be a hero. In fact, grovel like a loser.

"Hey, Logan," Nico said in a forced-casual voice. "What's going on? Nice ride."

"Of course it is," Logan snapped. "That's a Trailbreaker Extreme. It's the best."

Nico nodded like he was impressed, which, being honest, he was. Logan's dad owned the timber company and was the richest man in town. They used to be richer, but Nico's father had put a dent into that, an unpleasant fact Nico felt sure was about to come up unpleasantly.

"Are you guys scouting for exotic birds?" Logan smiled darkly. "Adding more precious species to the list?"

Nico held in a sigh. *It's never going away.*

"Look, Logan," Nico began, "I didn't—"

"Is this your drone?" Logan interrupted, pointing at the quadcopter.

Nico thought it was a ridiculous question, but he answered anyway. "Yes."

Logan bent down to give it a closer inspection. "Pretty nice! Can I have a turn?"

Oh no. Oh no oh no oh no.

Emma caught Nico's eye and shook her head. Tyler's

mouth twisted like he'd bitten into a lemon. But there was nothing Nico could do.

"Sure. Yeah. Just . . . you know . . ."

Logan rose slowly, holding Nico's eye. "Just . . . *what*, Nicolas?"

Nico swallowed. "Just be careful. The controls take a little getting used to."

Logan flashed perfect white teeth. "Don't worry, I can handle it."

He removed his driving gloves and held out a hand. Reluctantly, Nico passed him the remote. Everyone watched as Logan launched the quadcopter straight up into the air. A genuine smile broke out on his face as he guided it around the field in a huge circle, steering it back to hover over their heads. "This *is* pretty cool, Nico."

Nico released a pent-up breath. Maybe Logan honestly just wanted to fly the drone.

"I'm curious though," Logan said, rolling his shoulders. "Are drones as fast as owls?"

Before Nico could respond, Logan jabbed the controller. The drone sped straight for the fog above Still Cove.

"Wait!" Nico lunged for the remote, but Logan shoved him back at Carson, who seized his arms. Parker stared down Emma and Tyler. Helpless, Nico watched his drone disappear into the eddying mists.

"Who knows, Holland?" Logan dropped the controller

and kicked it away. "Maybe Still Cove is a protected breeding ground for crappy machines."

Nico scrambled after the remote as Logan strolled to his ATV. Nico glanced over his shoulder and found Opal watching him, her expression unreadable. But he didn't have time to consider it. He scooped up the controller and frantically tried to maneuver his drone back into the sky.

Laughter echoed as the riders mounted, fired their engines, and rode off. Nico desperately worked the switches, but minutes passed and nothing appeared.

Emma sniffed. Tyler put a hand on Nico's shoulder. "So sorry, man," he said quietly. "It must've dropped out of range. Those guys are the biggest jerks in the world."

Nico shook his head, anger and denial balling in his chest like melted chewing gum. "No. It's a Phantom! They float. It'll come back up once I reconnect." But repeated jabs on the remote had no effect.

Emma wiped her eyes. "Why were they out here, anyway? I was sure we'd be alone."

"They ride those stupid things everywhere," Tyler muttered. "Logan loves looking like a tough guy."

Nico refused to admit defeat. He rose and stomped toward the fog-covered cliff. "The problem is distance. I need to get closer. Then I'll catch the signal and everything will be fine."

"Dude!" Tyler's hand rose in a gesture of hopelessness. "That's Still Cove down there. We can't even see the water. It's gone, man. There's no way."

"I don't have to go all the way. Just far enough to link with the Phantom."

Nico began pacing the edge. The cliffs appeared sheer, without any easy places to descend, but twenty yards ahead Nico spotted a steeply angled ledge knifing into the fog. "Here! I can crawl along this until I'm low enough to link up again."

Tyler threw his hands skyward. "Nico, *stop*. You can't even see where that goes!"

"He's right," Emma said in a shaky voice. "That's not safe, Nico. Don't do it."

But Nico was already inching onto the ledge. "It's fine, guys. Really. I'll go extra slow. I'm not crazy."

"Then stop *acting* crazy!" Tyler actually stomped his foot. "You don't know how far that ledge goes, and you can't pilot the quad through that fog anyway. Get back here before you kill yourself!"

Ignoring Tyler, Nico shoved the remote into his hoodie pocket. He'd invested everything in that quadcopter. He wasn't going to let Logan Nantes take it from him. *No way.*

"Tyler, it's fine. The footing is good. If I take it one st—"

Pebbles crunched, followed by the shriek of rubber sliding on stone.

Nico's feet shot out from under him. He staggered sideways, arms pinwheeling. With a wide-eyed gasp, he looked back at his friends. Then Nico fell, disappearing into the mist.

He didn't even have time to scream.

2

OPAL

This isn't right.

As they rode away, Opal couldn't stop picturing Nico's face when his drone vanished into the mists. They'd been friends as little kids. He'd always liked building stuff. How long had he spent putting that machine together? How much had it cost?

"Stop," Opal said.

Logan glanced back over his shoulder. "What?" he yelled.

"I said, stop!"

Logan's eyes narrowed, but he hit the brakes and the ATV rolled to a halt. Opal pulled off the helmet he'd lent her. Logan removed his too, wiping muddy fingers through his hair. "What's wrong?"

Opal climbed from the ATV. The other machine idled behind them. "What's going on?" Parker shouted.

"I'm going back." Opal was already striding away.

"Back where?" When Opal didn't answer, Logan gunned the four-wheeler and swung around, coming to a stop directly in her path.

"You know where." Opal set her hands on her hips. "You shouldn't have done that."

She saw something harden in Logan's eyes, as often happened when people talked about Nico. At times, Logan could be fun. There were moments when Opal even thought he was cute. Not right now.

"I'm going to help them look," Opal said.

Carson snorted from atop the other four-wheeler. "That thing's *gone*, man. They'll never find it."

"It was probably expensive." Opal focused on Logan. Would he come along? She thought he liked her. He'd wanted to hang out all the time lately, ever since she'd moved from her old house to a few doors down from his home on Overlook Row.

But Logan shook his head, annoyed. "He cost my dad like a million times the price of that drone."

"His *father* did," Opal said, though she knew it was pointless. "Nico didn't do anything."

"Close enough." Logan put his helmet back on. "Come on, this is stupid."

Opal threw her helmet at Logan, forcing him to catch it awkwardly, and glanced at the other ATV. Carson smirked as he slapped down his visor. Parker shrugged.

She wasn't surprised. Opal was new to the group. After this, she might not be a part of it at all.

"Fine." Logan's tone was a mixture of frustration and resentment. "I guess you plan on walking back to town?"

"Guess so." Opal walked past him, the long grass brushing her legs. A rush of *I'm doing the right thing* washed over her. It lasted as the ATVs grumbled away. It lasted until she crested the final hill, and spotted Emma shouting while Tyler ripped at his hair.

Something was wrong.

Opal sprinted the last hundred yards, stopping just short of the cliff. "What happened?"

"Nico fell!" Tyler yelled, peering over the edge. He didn't even question what she was doing there.

A cold pit opened in Opal's stomach. "Into the cove?!"

Tyler nodded. His mouth worked, but nothing more came out.

"Did you call 911?" Opal yanked out her battered phone. "Or anyone?!"

"No coverage," Emma moaned, eyes shell-shocked. "Not until Razor Point!"

Emma was right—no bars. Panic washed over Opal. No one had ever fallen into Still Cove before. Not that she'd heard of, and she'd lived in Timbers her whole life. "We have to get down there," she said. "*Now.*"

"There's *no way* down!" Tyler moaned, wiping red-rimmed

eyes as he stared into the mist. "That's how Nico fell in the first place. He was trying to get to his drone."

"Then we'll *make* a way down," Opal fired back. "Unless you're not willing to try?"

Tyler flinched, but Opal's anger seemed to snap Emma out of her paralysis. "A rescue mission," she whispered. "Right. Let's hurry."

Trying not to freak out, Opal led Emma along the cliff's edge. Tyler trailed them.

"Be careful. It's slick up here," Opal warned, scanning the sheer-sided drop. "But there's got to be a way to the bottom. Like a game trail? Maybe animals go down to drink."

"Drink what?" Tyler countered, head down as he followed. "The salt water?"

"Just look for a path!" Opal snapped.

They scoured the hillside, pulling back shrubs and stringy branches, cursing when the ground slumped beneath their feet. It was eerie being this close to Still Cove. Like a cold breath on the back of your neck.

She tried not to think about what each second meant for Nico.

He can swim, can't he? Of course he can.

But Still Cove had no beach. No way out. And what lurked at the bottom?

What if he didn't hit the water? What if it wasn't deep enough?

17

"Look!" Emma pointed behind a lone pine sentinel. A barely-there dirt track cut along the inside of the bluff. Opal spotted the upside-down heart shapes of deer tracks.

Hallelujah.

"I'll go first," said Opal. "Are either of you coming?"

She didn't wait for an answer, slinking out onto the slender path before she lost her nerve. A beat later Opal heard two sets of footsteps following. She didn't look behind her. She couldn't. The trail descended steeply for a dozen yards before the fog covered everything.

"Nico?" Opal called. The mist seemed to swallow her voice whole. Something swished the branches of a tree clinging to the cliff wall. Opal's blood pressure spiked. What if it was Nico?

The movement came again, barely visible in the fog. Leaves parted and an owl scowled down at her, perturbed to find humans in its domain. "You started this," Opal hissed. "You and your endangeredness." The owl turned its head away.

"Opal?" Emma shouted from above. "You okay?"

"Yes." She could hear Emma, but the mist was relentless. Scree dribbled past her ankles as someone shifted higher up the trail. "Getting down is the hard part," Opal assured them, trying to sound confident. "Climbing back up will be easier." Then her own foot slid out from under her, carving a line through mud and soggy pine needles.

Her spirits sank. If Nico was hurt, how could they possibly carry him back up?

Find him first.

That's what her dad would say. He always stayed calm in a crisis, even lately, when his daily mail route included delivering eviction notices and overdue bills. Opal turned sideways and continued inching forward. The trail sunk deeper into the fog. Then all at once, she dipped below the mists.

"I see the bottom!" Opal shouted, eyeing the flat, mirror-like surface of Still Cove twenty yards farther down. The dark ocean seemed more ominous than the fog. "We're almost there."

"What about Nico?" Tyler yelled from above.

"Not yet." Opal breathed a sigh of relief at not seeing the broken body of Nico Holland cradled on any of the jagged rocks below. She hurried along the last of the trail to a shelf hanging a dozen feet above the water. Tyler and Emma crashed down after her.

The ledge was six yards wide and three deep. A cave burrowed into the cliff face behind it. Opal stepped inside and spotted a crack in the roof with water trickling through it, spilling down to form a shallow, sandy pool. *That's what the deer come for. But the path ends here.*

"Nico must've landed in the cove," Tyler said, leading them back out onto the ledge. "That's good news, at least."

"Then where *is* he?" Emma glanced around in a state of

near-panic. "The walls are vertical. There's nowhere from him to climb out!"

Opal kept her voice steady. "He must still be swimming around, then."

"NICO!" Emma bellowed, cupping her hands over her lips. "Nico, where are you?!"

"*Shhh*," Tyler hissed, waving madly for quiet. "Don't forget we're in Still Cove right now. *For real*. Think about what that means!"

Opal stared. "Please tell me you're not talking about the Beast."

"Laugh all you want," Tyler scolded. "Right until it snatches us off this ledge."

There was no response to Emma's call. She stormed back into the cave. "Maybe he's in here somewhere."

Opal peered across the inlet, goosebumps spreading at the thought of touching that murky water. How must Nico have felt, dropping into it from the top of the cliff? Was there *any* chance he was okay?

"Guys!" Emma's voice echoed behind Opal. "There's more cave!"

"Is Nico in there?" Opal asked, spinning around. But even in the gloom she saw Emma's shoulders slump.

"No," Emma grumbled, dejected. "Just some old junk."

"Junk?" Opal hurried to join her. At first she couldn't make out anything in the gloom, but then she spotted a darker shadow in the black and slipped forward to inspect it. "A rowboat!"

A thick weave of spiderwebs coated the battered vessel, but it seemed to be in one piece. "Look, oars!" Opal grabbed a gunwale and began dragging the boat toward the ledge. "We can use this to look for Nico."

"Why is this boat here?" Tyler demanded. "In a deserted cave in the middle of nowhere?"

"Who knows, but we're taking it. We'll push it into the cove and jump in after." Opal's patience was running out. How much longer could Nico tread water?

Emma nodded, grabbing the other paddle.

"Jump in the water," Tyler said slowly. "The water where the Beast lives." He pressed both palms to his eye sockets. "Guys, we don't have life jackets. You're not supposed to get into a boat without a life jacket."

Opal slapped the hull, eyes fierce. "Nico doesn't have one either, Tyler. *Or* a boat."

"Thanks to you and your friends!" Tyler shot back, his face a twist of worry and fear. He backed against the cliff, eyes roving for an escape.

Opal flinched. It was true. She hated what Logan had done, hated everything about the crappy situation except this lifeline of a boat. "You're right. I'll go alone."

"I'm in." Emma took a deep breath. "Nico would do it for me."

Opal tried to not show her relief. "Let's hurry."

Together they shoved the rowboat over the edge. It hit the water with a heavy *thwack*.

"Here we go." Opal exhaled slowly, shaking out her limbs. "No big deal. No big deal."

With an oar tucked under her arm, she stepped off the ledge.

———————————

Slap-cold, breath gone.

Opal's body shrieked with the shock of the icy water. She sank like a stone, feeling the cove surge over her. Swallowing her.

She heard a splash nearby. *Emma?*

And another. *Tyler?*

Or was that something else?

Opal surfaced. The boat was ahead, bobbing right side up, appearing seaworthy despite its peeling boards. Opal swam awkwardly, dragging the oar, the water so frigid she couldn't call out.

Opal hauled herself aboard, being careful not to capsize the vessel. A moment later a slender hand grabbed the opposite rail. Opal helped Emma scramble up into the boat.

"W-where's your o-oar?" Opal chattered as Emma collapsed into a ball, her blond hair soaked and dripping.

"I've got it!" Tyler shouted from somewhere near the stern.

"Get me out! *Oh please*, get me out! I think something's in here with me!"

The top of a paddle appeared. Opal wobbled forward and snagged it. Together with Emma, they pulled Tyler up as he half climbed, half somersaulted to safety.

"We made it," Opal breathed. She fit her oar in a worn bracket and dipped its blade into the glass-like water. "Let's go."

Emma rubbed the back of her neck. "Sure, but where to?"

Opal shrugged, anxious to be *doing* rather than thinking. "Around. In circles. Back and forth. I don't know, but we need to *find Nico*."

"One of the greatest plans ever formed," Tyler muttered, but he fit the second oar.

Emma moved to a lookout position in the bow and, slowly, gracelessly, the boat slid forward. It took Tyler and Opal a minute to find their rhythm, but soon they were pulling in time, gliding across the water.

"Nico!" Emma shouted. "Nico, where are you?!"

Tyler winced with every call, but didn't bring up the Beast again. "Should we stick close to shore, or crisscross the inlet?" he asked.

"I don't know," Opal admitted. Up close, the cove was dark and murky, with strange sounds and odd ripples. Shadows moved in the corner of her eye. The fog swirled everywhere.

Tyler grunted. "We're already headed toward the center, so maybe keep going? Nico might hear us sooner."

Opal glanced up, then did a double take, nearly losing her oar. Emma shouted at the same moment, pointing to a dark shape looming in the leaden half-light.

An island rose out of the mists, ringed with brooding forest.

Opal had never heard anyone mention an island in Still Cove before.

Nico. Surely he'd have gone for that.

Tyler swallowed, half rising from his bench to stare. "Does . . . does that look like the kind of place where a giant sea monster might live?"

Emma sucked on her teeth. "It looks like where King Kong lives."

Icy fingers traced down Opal's spine. Her heart sped up as something sang through her, like the echo of a strange note. This island felt . . . wild. Untamed. Unknowable. Every instinct in her body sounded the alarm at once.

"If I were stuck in the water," Opal said, "that's where I'd go."

"Dry land." Tyler couldn't tear his eyes from it. "Yeah. He'd go there."

"Then what are we waiting for?" Opal plunged her oar into the slate-colored seawater. Tyler did the same, and the boat swept forward on silent wings.

24

3

NICO

Nico spat out a mouthful of sand.

He collapsed onto his back, exhausted and soaked with frigid seawater. Then he rolled over and threw up. When he'd finished heaving, Nico pushed up with his arms and squinted, choking back a spike of panic. He dug his fingers into the beach, confirming that it was solid, that he could stand on it, and that he wasn't going to drown.

He'd made it to the island, but it had been *close*.

Stupid! Stupid stupid stupid.

He'd fallen into Still Cove! From the top of the cliff!

Nico had barely had time to realize he was going to die before being swallowed by the fog and then spit out into dark, freezing water. The impact had knocked him senseless. It was a freaking *miracle* he'd managed to claw back to the surface.

That's when terror set in. Vertical walls surrounding him. Unknown depths below. Nico had grown convinced he'd survived the fall only to swim in helpless circles until he sank. He'd blundered into a floating log by pure luck. Adrift and alone, he'd very nearly given up. Until the island appeared, rising from the mists like a smear of midnight.

He'd ditched the slimy log and swam for land, icy seawater numbing his limbs, fighting to pull him down. At one point he felt the horrible sensation of something large moving beneath him, but he pushed through, crawling from the ocean and kissing the dirty sand.

And now . . . here he was.

Something jabbed his side. Nico untwisted his drenched hoodie and pulled out the drone's remote. It was cracked and dripping wet. Nico dropped the ruined controller with a sigh.

He rose and faced the mist-cloaked island. Its narrow beach curved away on both sides. Straight ahead, a dark forest climbed into the fog and out of sight. Nico shivered. Literally every option seemed bad, but he definitely wasn't getting back into the water.

Nico ran a hand through his sodden hair, spiking it with his fingers. He needed a plan, but nothing came to mind. Tyler and Emma were trapped on the cliff top and probably freaking out. His dad was out of town. The closest boats were all the way back in Timbers. Nico was hungry and thirsty and tired. Worst of all, the quadcopter was nowhere in sight.

All for nothing. Nico kicked a rock into the water. What

had he done to deserve this? They'd been minding their own business, flying the drone. Logan was such a jerk.

Don't forget Opal. She watched and did nothing, then rode off like Nico didn't exist. If he'd ever doubted their friendship was dust, now he had proof. She was just like the others.

"Enough." Nico spoke out loud to underline the point. "You're wasting daylight."

He looked up and down the beach. It didn't encourage exploration. Nico peered into the fog-soaked woods. How high did the island rise? Maybe if he climbed up, he could see more of the cove. Find a way out.

A way out how? You think there's a bus station up there?

Nico shoved the negative thought away. Nothing on the empty beach would help his situation. Going somewhere, *anywhere*, felt better than standing there and shivering.

He'd taken two steps when he heard his name. Low and ghostly, it floated on the wind. He whirled to face the water, eyes rounding. All the horror stories about Still Cove came screaming back to him.

Nico froze, ears straining. But after a tense minute, he relaxed. Even cracked a smile. *My mind is playing tricks on me.* But the smile vanished when his name repeated, louder and closer, echoing from everywhere and nowhere at once.

Nico stumbled back. Goosebumps erupted along his arms. He had a very serious concern he might wet his pants.

Out on the water, a long shadow pierced the fog. The silhouette coalesced into the shape of a rowboat. As Nico gaped, a tiny form materialized at its head.

Nico blinked. Blinked again.

He recognized the figure in the bow. It was . . . Emma.

———————

Emma hit the sand running, tackling Nico in a flying bear hug. Tyler arrived an instant later and the trio bounced in a chattering, jubilant circle. It took Nico a minute to notice a third person, pulling the rowboat onto the beach alone.

"*Opal?*" Nico whispered.

Tyler released Nico with a slug to his shoulder. "Her idea, dude. I freaked out up there, but Emma found a path and Opal led the way." Tyler trotted over to help Opal with the boat.

Nico shook his head. He was touched—he couldn't believe they'd climbed down after him. "What's she even doing here?"

"She came back." Emma still clutched his arm. "By *herself*. She ditched Logan and the others."

Before Nico could process this, Opal was in front of him. Their eyes met, but neither spoke. An awkward silence swallowed the beach. Finally, Opal broke it.

"I'm glad you're okay."

"Thanks." Nico's cheeks burned for some reason. "Thanks, um . . . for coming after me. For trying to make up for things."

Nico regretted the words as soon as he said them. Opal

turned away, mumbling about checking the oars. Nico started to apologize, but stopped. Why should *he* say sorry? This wasn't his fault. Opal was part of the reason they were all stuck down there, dripping wet, on an uncharted island in the middle of Still Cove.

"Did you see the drone anywhere?" Tyler asked, blowing out a snot-rocket.

Nico glanced at his friend, momentarily thrown. "What? No. I didn't see it."

Emma was gazing into the shadowy woods. "Did anyone else know there was an island down here? I've never heard a story about one."

"Me neither," Tyler said. "How big do you think it is?"

Nico sighed, the energy leaking out of him like a popped balloon. "I haven't seen more than you have. I spent our time apart swimming for my life." He couldn't keep the resentment out of his voice as he darted a glance at Opal.

Opal dropped the oar she was holding and spun to face him. "Look, Nico, I didn't fly your toy into the cove, all right? *Logan* did that. I'm the one who came back to help. This isn't my fault, so you can stop going after me."

Nico's own temper slipped. "If you feel guilty about something, that's your problem." He turned to Tyler, but spoke loud enough for Opal to hear. "No, Ty, I haven't seen my quad-copter. I'll probably never find it. But at least I got to fall off a cliff and nearly drown instead."

Opal huffed, seemed ready for more, but Emma stepped between them. "Maybe it's not lost, though. Logan flew the drone directly into the fog, right?"

Nico took a calming breath before addressing his friend. "Yes. So?"

"So maybe it landed here." Emma waved at the trees. "This feels like the center of the cove. The quad could be just up the hill somewhere, safe and sound."

Nico was about to argue—*what are the odds?*—but Tyler cut him off. "We might as well go look. We've got a boat, but we don't know where we are." He frowned at the fog. "Let's climb to higher ground and see what we can see. Otherwise, we could paddle around for hours and still not find a way out of the cove."

Nico glanced at the woods. He didn't have much hope for the drone, yet as he stared at the forest, he felt an odd pull. He shivered, even as a thrill ran through him.

Then Opal stomped past him, heading directly for the woods. "Well?" she called over her shoulder. "The light won't last forever." She reached the first row of gnarled trunks and slipped between them.

"I do *not* understand girls," Tyler muttered.

Nico nodded mutely.

"Because you're both doofuses," Emma said brightly. "Opal's right, though."

Nico squeezed the bridge of his nose. "Come on. She'll

probably find the quad sitting on a pedestal, and we'll never live it down."

Ten feet in, the forest gloom enveloped them. Nico tripped on a root and nearly tumbled into a stream. Shaking water from his sneaker, he pointed to a heel print in the mud. "Opal's following this creek. Let's hurry. The last thing we need is for anyone to get lost."

The woods began to thin as they followed the stream. Nico caught up to Opal on a rocky crease poking above the tree line. He nodded to her awkwardly, then glanced away, gazing back the way they'd come. He could see only misty treetops, with glimpses of the beach below.

Without a word, Opal resumed climbing. Together they scrambled over broken boulders covered in wet pine needles, cursing scrapes and a skinned knee. Nico ripped off his hoodie and left it on a moss-covered rock. At the top of the ridge, Opal wobbled upright, peering down at the other side. Her eyes widened and she gasped.

Nico joined her, following her line of sight. "Oh, wow."

In the center of the island was a pond—a blue-black circle of darkness that swallowed the light around it. Nothing reflected off its surface. The water lay flat and still.

The pond was unsettling. It looked like a hole in the world.

And there was something floating *on* the pond.

"It's a . . . house," Opal said, at the exact moment Nico asked, "Is that a boat?"

The gray-planked structure rose two stories, with grimy windows and a wide front porch. It looked regal and dilapidated at the same time, as if a fancy hotel had grown from the water and been left to rot.

The ancient houseboat—for Nico abruptly realized that's what it was—seemed both dead and . . . strangely alive. As if it waited for something.

Emma and Tyler clambered up next to them and the foursome clustered atop the same flat rock.

They all stared, words stolen from their lips.

The pull Nico felt earlier returned.

Come inside, the building seemed to whisper.

Come and see what I have for you.

4

OPAL

Come and see what I have for you.

Opal shot a glance at the others, but they were all staring at the houseboat. A strange smile tilted the corners of Nico's mouth. "Hey," Opal began, but the word caught in her throat.

"Should we go inside?" Emma's eyes sparkled, even as she shivered.

Lips pursed, Tyler shook his head. "Nope. *No way.* That's how we die. Right there on that boat." A gust rattled the tree branches behind them and he jumped.

"We could die right here, too." Opal rubbed her arms. "Of hypothermia."

Nico shot her a look. "No one's dying. But we might as well go check it out. Maybe that building has a map."

"Or dry clothes," Opal said.

"Or pirate treasure." Emma started down the hill.

Tyler muttered something about prime Beast hideouts, but

he followed after her. Opal and Nico caught up on a long grassy field that bordered the water. Stark and imposing, the houseboat lurked at the center of the pond.

"I'm not swimming in that," said Tyler. "No chance."

"No need." Opal pointed farther up the shore. A line of flat gray stones were scattered across the pond, like a game of hopscotch leading to the houseboat.

"Great." Tyler heaved a sigh. "Just great." They circled to the stones. Emma leaped onto the first one, extending her arms for balance. "Come on. I'm the shortest. If I can make it, everyone can."

"It's not a matter of *can*," Tyler grumbled. "It's about *should*." But to Opal's surprise he jumped next, landing on the first rock as Emma hopped to the second.

"Go ahead," Nico said to Opal.

"Such a gentleman." She bit off the words. "But I don't mind being last."

Nico rolled his eyes and followed Tyler. Opal waited until he was halfway across before starting after him. She couldn't explain why she was so mad, but that didn't make it go away. "Hurry up, you guys!" Emma waved from the boat's front porch.

As Opal reached the last stone, Nico held out a hand to help her up. She took it, not wanting to fall. His fingers were warm despite the frosty air and their wet clothes. The rickety steps of the houseboat crunched with splintered wood and dead leaves. Opal worried her foot might go right through. *What is this place?*

"Take a look at this." Tyler pointed to the entrance. "Weird, right?" The door was made of wood framing a thick pane of warped, foggy glass with air bubbles trapped inside. Opal couldn't see through it.

"A glass door on a boat?" Nico's mouth twisted. "Who thought that was a good idea?"

Emma stepped forward and tried the knob. It didn't budge.

Tyler clapped his hands together. "*Welp*. Guess we should leave it alone, then."

Opal joined Emma and they tried together. The knob finally turned with a screech and the girls forced the door inward with their shoulders. Scents of decay rushed out to greet them.

Opal took a tentative step into the dusty foyer. Ahead was a cobwebbed archway covered by a green velvet curtain. She heard the door close behind her.

"Oh, wow," Emma whispered. "Way cool. Like our own *Night at the Museum*."

"People got hurt in those movies," Tyler mumbled darkly, but even he seemed awed.

Opal crossed to the heavy curtain and pushed it aside. Her breath caught.

An enormous room opened up before her, lit by grimy glass skylights. Broken sunshine slanted through them, illuminating a haphazard assortment of strange objects. Paintings. Wooden chests loaded with crusty books. Knickknacks of every shape and size. Old photographs hung in crooked frames along the walls, some of them broken. A jumble of antique weapons filled an open coffin beside the door.

"Whoa." Emma bit down on her thumbnail. An animal's skeleton dangled from the ceiling, knotty bones wound and spiraling in a loop, ending with an elongated skull. Opal lifted the yellowing placard affixed to its tail, but the ink had faded away.

"This isn't a museum," Tyler muttered, sounding queasy. "We're in a psychopath's attic."

"It's definitely some kind of collection." Nico brushed a fraying red rope strung between two tarnished poles.

They wandered down a center aisle dividing the overstuffed room. Emma pointed to a crate with *Mummy* branded on its side. Inside was something shriveled and brown, curled up as if avoiding their eyes.

"Looks like jerky," Nico said, peering closer.

"*Ugh.*" Opal pinched her lips together. Did he have to be so disgusting?

"We could eat it to survive," Emma said cheerfully. When Opal stared at her, she shrugged. "What? In this movie I saw, *Natural Selection*, they totally did that."

"Never heard of it," Opal said.

"Most people haven't. But it's really good. Well, not *good* so much as gross."

"Whoa, check *this* out." Tyler was staring into an iron-banded chest filled with twinkling gemstones. "Any way these puppies are real?"

Nico grinned wickedly. "If so, we're rich!"

"You want to rob the place?" Opal couldn't believe it. They'd found a storehouse full of amazing, awesome things, and he was talking about *stealing* them?

"We don't all live on Overlook Row," Nico muttered.

Opal bit her lip. She used to live a block from Nico, but when his dad made a federal case about those owls, people lost their jobs. That allowed her parents to snag the big yellow house they'd wanted for years. Her mother had foreclosed on the property herself as part of her work at the bank.

In fact, Opal's moving was kind of *Nico's* fault, if you thought about it. At the very least, it was his dad's.

Opal crossed the showroom floor in search of another door. Cool or not, the place was also starting to give her the creeps, like a wax museum she'd been to once in San Francisco. It felt like everything was watching her.

A pedestal near the back of the chamber caught her attention. Atop it sat a large jar with something green floating inside. Curious, Opal walked over to investigate.

"What's that?" Emma asked, following along. "One of those old lava lamps?"

"I don't know." Emma's description was a good one. Inside the bulky jar was . . . *something*. A shifting, lime-colored blob.

On impulse, Opal pressed a finger to the glass, like she used to do at the aquarium when she was little.

"What the heck?" Nico asked, joining them. Emma grabbed his arm, her face flushing with excitement. "Nico, this is the coolest place on Earth, and no one else knows about it. I claim this houseboat for *us*. Me, you, and Ty—we have a clubhouse now!" She bounced on the balls of her feet, eyes alight.

Opal's stomach knotted. *Me too, right?*

The thought surprised her. Was that what she wanted? A weird hideout five miles from town, shared with three kids she never hung out with, or even talked to much?

Yes, she realized. Almost all summer she'd been tagging along with Logan and his friends. Hoping for . . . *something* to happen. Anything new or different. And now she'd found it.

Opal glanced at Nico, and found him watching her. Before she could think of what to say, Tyler called out from across the room. "Yo! Genius Boy over here found a map of Still Cove. It shows how we can paddle out of this nightmare." He sauntered down the aisle with a scroll in his hands.

"Time to go," Nico said, and Opal felt a door slam shut between them. "My dad gets home tonight, and he'll freak out if I miss dinner."

"*Boooo.*" Emma moaned. "Okay, fine. But we *are* coming back. Like, tomorrow, right?" She nodded in answer to her own question before glancing at Opal, eyes curious. Not inviting, but not rude either.

Nico snorted. "Like we could stop you."

"Back into the cove again." Tyler rubbed his eyes. "Mercy. Let's just get this boat ride over with."

"It'll be fine." Nico pushed Tyler's shoulder. "Nothing ate us the first time, right?"

Tyler groaned, but Emma giggled. Even Opal cracked a smile. They all headed for the door, leaving behind a herd of dusty footprints and a swirling, mist-green jar.

5

NICO

Breakfast was cold cereal again.

Nico didn't mind. He liked cereal, and his father knew enough to stock more than one box when he went away. But the milk had gone bad, so Nico had to eat it dry. It was better than nothing.

He glanced at the calendar tacked to the kitchen wall. His brother had gone to Gonzaga this year and wouldn't be home until Thanksgiving, which was both a relief and a drag. Rob could be moody—he liked to rub Nico's face into the carpet as a joke—but he also used to make the backup grocery runs. Now Nico had to do it.

They'll all stare at me in the supermarket. Whispering. That'll be fun.

Nico shook off the unpleasant thought. There was nothing he could do about it.

He put his bowl in the sink, grabbed his brother's old

Sonics pullover—*his* pullover now—and slid into his ratty backpack. Shutting off the TV in the small den, he left by the side door, making sure to lock it behind him.

His father had been due back last night, but he'd spotted something up by the timberline that needed checking out. At least, that's what his text message said. No big deal. Nico got himself ready for school every day anyway.

His mom had died when he was three and he didn't remember much about her. Just feeling loved and warm, a kind voice, and sometimes a gentle face. He avoided pictures of his mother because he didn't want to replace that. The memories were flawed, but they were *his*. Nico wanted to keep it that way.

They were just the Holland boys for years, one big and two little. But now Rob was gone and his dad worked all the time. Lately, Nico felt like he was on his own.

The wind outside had turned cold. Next door, Mr. Murphy was sweeping leaves off his front porch. Their eyes met as Nico walked by, and he felt the old man's glower burn into him. Nico looked away, hurrying toward the sidewalk. Mr. Murphy had been a shift foreman at the mill before the layoffs. He wasn't now.

It was seven blocks to Timbers Middle School. Lately, it felt like a million. Not everyone was as hostile as Mr. Murphy, but neighbors watched him from their bungalows with closed-off faces. Nobody called down hellos anymore. Nico began to breathe easier once he reached the park three streets down. The rolling fields and evergreen trees were an oasis of calm before the even rockier shore of the school yard.

He'd lived here all his life. Timbers was a quiet little mill town, nestled between the bluffs of Skagit Sound. There were three big roads and two traffic lights, with everything running along Otter Creek down to the docks. Too remote to be a true tourist destination, Timbers relied on ferry traffic to keep its businesses open, though it was often a struggle. Things had gotten worse since the mill cutbacks, but Nico tried not to think about that.

He was always trying not to think about that.

Nico spotted the school ahead, and his spirits dropped again. He glanced right, down a steep lane plunging toward the docks, and left, at a dirt road climbing into the mountains. Either option would be better than going to school. Hiking, fishing, scanning for birds. Whatever. But his father would crush him if he skipped school. Warren Holland didn't understand how it was for Nico, or he chose not to care. Nico couldn't decide which was worse.

Heaving an enormous sigh, he hitched his pack and headed into battle.

He avoided the playground crowd and slipped into the building, beelining to his locker. For once there were no nasty surprises inside. Nico grabbed his physical science textbook. It was his favorite subject, and Mr. Huang was the one teacher who seemed openly sympathetic to his predicament.

He closed his locker. Wheeled around. And nearly barged into Opal.

Had she been waiting behind him? Or was it pure coincidence?

"Hey, Nico." Opal's hand rose to tangle itself in her shimmering black hair. As a kid Nico had been fascinated by Opal's hair, though he'd usually expressed it by yanking on her braid and giggling as she slugged him for it. That was a long time ago.

"Hey," he said back. The uncomfortable moment stretched as they both examined their shoes. Nico cleared his throat, but nothing followed.

"Are you going back to the houseboat later?" Opal blurted.

Nico shrugged, uncertain how to answer. "I haven't talked to the others yet, but I know Emma wants to. So, I guess . . ." He trailed off, and Opal made no effort to fill the dead air again. Nico realized they hadn't spoken in the hallway all that year, and maybe not the year before that, either. He wasn't sure he wanted to. The image of her on Logan's four-wheeler played in his head. Was she a friend at all?

"Nico, I want to—"

She didn't get a chance to finish. As if summoned by Nico's thoughts, Logan appeared behind her, with Carson and Parker looming at his back.

Nico ground his teeth. He'd been close to a clean getaway that morning, but Opal had ruined it.

"Captain Holland!" Logan saluted, prompting snickers

from his flunkies. "Sorry about the drone yesterday. I'm so bad at flying things. I'm like a . . . a *bird* brain, you know?"

A weak-sauce taunt, and Nico was tempted to mock Logan for it, but he held his tongue. Logan would just start in some other way. The safest bet was to keep his mouth shut and wait for the bell.

Nico glanced at Opal, but she was staring at the linoleum. *Some friend.*

"I hope it wasn't expensive." Logan's eyes cut to Opal to make sure she was listening. "But I have a replacement for you." He pulled a paper airplane from his textbook and unfolded its flimsy wings. "You can pilot this now, see? Zoom, zoom!"

Logan flicked his fingers and the plane arrowed at Nico's face, forcing him to bat it aside. Carson and Parker exploded in laughter. Nico's hands balled into fists. He imagined how good it would feel to slam one into Logan's smirking mouth.

Nico caught Opal watching him. He saw pity there, which made him feel even worse. For a terrifying moment Nico worried he might start crying in front of her. He lowered his head and took a step down the hall, but Logan stopped him with a hand.

This is never going to end. Not ever.

Logan cocked his head. "Something wrong, Birdman? Are your feathers ruffled?"

"Logan, *enough*," Opal hissed.

Logan's head whipped to her, eyes narrowing. Nico used the distraction to push past him and escape down the hall.

"Catch you later, Eagle Scout!" Parker called after him.

As Nico turned a corner, he saw Logan and Opal speaking in low voices. Carson and Parker hung a few paces back, playing who-can-shove-the-other-harder. Nico stormed out of sight.

Twenty seconds later, he was safely in Mr. Huang's class. Emma and Tyler were waiting at the workstation the three of them shared. Their conversation broke off as Nico sat heavily and slammed his book onto the table.

Tyler scowled. "Logan, huh?"

"I don't want to talk about it."

"We could pour water in his fuel tank?" Emma suggested, mimicking handlebars with her hands. "ATV no more go."

"I said I don't want to talk about it." Nico was a weird mix of angry and embarrassed. "Just leave it alone, okay?" His pulse was slowing, but his stomach still hurt. He thought of Opal buddying around with those jerks, and his lips curled in disgust.

"Is there anything we can do?" Emma asked softly.

Nico sighed, putting a hand over his eyes. "No. But thanks."

"We're still going to the island after school, right?" Emma batted puppy dog eyes. "*Please?* You can count it as my birthday present. For the next seven years."

Nico couldn't help but laugh. "Fine. But we have to be back by dark. My dad won't flake out two nights in a row."

"What do you think that houseboat really is?" Tyler glanced around to make sure that no one was listening in. "How the heck did it get there? Because I've got a bad feeling about a floating collection of misfit toys nobody seems to be watching."

"It's a mystery," Emma agreed, but in an entirely different tone. "We have to solve it!"

"I'm curious, too." Nico lifted a hand to cut Tyler off. "We'll just take another look. And you know you want to, so stop playing around. We're the only people on Earth who know about that place."

"Going into Still Cove on purpose." Tyler shook his head as Emma raised her arms in triumph. "How stupid can we be?"

"Don't tell Opal," Nico said sharply. "Don't tell her anything we're doing, period."

Tyler shrugged. Emma frowned, but nodded. The bell rang and they faced forward as Mr. Huang closed the hallway door.

Another day to get through, Nico thought. *One hour at a time.*

6

OPAL

They ditched me.

Opal stood at the mouth of the cave.

No Nico, Emma, or Tyler. And, when she peered down at the water, no rowboat.

Only a few daylight hours remained, and her parents would miss her soon. Did she have time to get her dad's canoe? Could she paddle all the way back to Still Cove, or even find the island again if she did?

Why'd they leave me behind?

The day before, they'd tied the rowboat to a sunken post below the cave, promising to keep everything secret. It was *Opal* who'd spotted hidden notches carved into the cliff, which let them climb up to the ledge from the water.

They'd done it all as a group. *Together.*

And then they ditched her.

She'd looked for the others after school, then pedaled to

the field and found three bikes in a pile. So she'd descended the heart-stopping trail through the fog and discovered exactly what she'd feared. She was alone.

Tears burned behind Opal's eyelids, but she blinked them back. She walked into the cave and splashed water on her face. When she finished, she kicked at the stone wall, dirtying her sneakers. They were *not* going to cut her out of this. Suddenly furious, Opal kicked the wall again. Dirt rained down on her head. *Stupid. Don't make the roof fall in on you.*

She had to think. How could she get to the island?

We found one boat in this cave. Maybe there's another?

Opal moved deeper, exploring the narrow fissure where the rowboat had been. Near the back, a draft chilled her skin. With a start, Opal realized there was a hidden corner. *A passageway.* Her phone light was just bright enough to reach the next turn.

Opal stared into the opening for a dozen heartbeats. Opal took a deep breath. *Why not?*

She entered a narrow tunnel reeking of seawater and damp earth. The path dove sharply, switching back and forth as it burrowed underground. After dozens of turns, the way leveled. A long, straight tunnel stretched out before her. Water dripped from its ceiling.

Fear squeezed Opal's throat. A warning of *Go back!* coursed through her, shouted down by a second voice that whispered: *This might take you where you want to go.* She tried not to think about the thousands of tons of rock and seawater above her head. The tunnel had to cut directly underneath the cove.

Gritting her teeth, Opal ran headlong into the pitch black.

Just keep moving. This has to lead somewhere.

At one point the passage widened into an open space, but Opal raced through it until the walls narrowed again. She *had* to find the others. She was tired of being the odd one out, the afterthought. She was an outsider to her parents' lives, their jobs at work and their obsession with the new house. And she was an interloper in Logan's group. He kept inviting her places, but she knew Parker and Carson resented it. Ever since her best friend Melissa moved to Seattle last year, Opal felt that she was hovering at the edge of everyone else's closed circles. And now this.

The tunnel ended at the bottom of a jagged ramp. Opal jogged up another set of switchbacks to a second, smaller cave. Outside, brambles choked the bottom of a steep-sided gully.

Opal knew where she was. She'd been right.

She was standing on the island in Still Cove.

Opal climbed up the ridge. From the top, she could see the dark wound of the pond and its eerie houseboat.

Opal grinned wickedly.

She had a secret.

———

Opal pushed open the front door of the houseboat, strode through the foyer, and parted the velvet curtain. She found the others crouched over an old wooden trunk.

"Hi, everyone."

It was almost worth being left behind.

Tyler's eyes popped.

Emma's mouth dropped open in amazement.

Nico straightened like a switchblade. "What are you doing here?"

"I have as much right to be here as you do." Opal spoke calmly, though her heart thudded inside her chest. "You should've invited me to come with you."

"How'd you *get* here?" Emma seemed more astonished than upset.

"I have my ways," Opal replied, trying to be cryptic and casual all at once. *Make them wonder.*

Tyler raised his eyebrows like he was impressed, but Nico replied bitterly. "We didn't invite you on purpose. You can't barge in and tell us what to do."

"*You* can't keep me out," Opal shot back.

Tyler began edging down the aisle. "So I'm just gonna . . . head on over . . . away from here. Maybe I'll look for a bathroom." He shot a glance at Emma. "You want to help?"

Emma shook her head. "No thanks. I went before we came."

Tyler covered his face with his hand. "Emma . . ."

Odd she didn't take the hint, Opal thought. Tyler

and Emma had been joined at the hip since second grade, when Emma's family moved to Timbers and opened a tiny sporting goods store. *Why is she sticking around now? Hoping to see some fireworks?* Opal could not figure her out.

"You're not a part of our group." Nico crossed his arms, refusing to look directly at Opal. "This place doesn't change that."

Ouch. Opal thought about all the times she and Nico had played as kids, building pillow forts in Nico's den, or camping out in Opal's backyard. Sometimes they'd race their bikes around the fountain in town square until they got dizzy, screaming that a black hole had gotten them. They'd collapse on the grass and take turns imagining new worlds on the other side of the galaxy.

This houseboat was as close to a new world as Opal might ever find.

Nico Holland was not going to ruin it for her.

Her nostrils flared. "Listen. I don't want to argue with you, but—"

"Holy crap!" Tyler yelled, but he wasn't anywhere in sight. His voice sounded muffled, as if it were coming from behind another room. "Yo, check this out!"

"Knock it off, Ty," Nico shouted. "Nobody wants to hear about your . . . business."

"Not a bathroom." Tyler's head popped from behind a wall panel. "Something even weirder."

Emma startled. "Where'd you come from?"

Tyler waggled his eyebrows. "I found a trick panel. I think there's a basement."

"Boats don't have basements," Nico shot back.

"*This* one does. Get over here!" Tyler ducked back out of sight.

"Secret door!" Emma squealed, clapping her hands as she raced across the room.

Opal brushed past Nico, ignoring his intake of breath as she stepped around the weird jar pedestal. She belonged there, whatever Nico thought. He couldn't close her out of this. *I won't allow it.*

The wall's wooden panels fit snugly together, but when Opal pressed on the section where Tyler had been, it popped open to reveal a wrought-iron spiral staircase.

"Whoa." Emma turned on her phone light and aimed it at the steps.

Tyler had stopped a quarter turn down and seemed to be listening.

"This must be where they keep the good stuff!" Emma hopped onto the steps.

"*Wait.*" Tyler held out an arm to stop her. "Should we make sure it's safe first?"

"That's what I'm doing." Emma sidled past him down the stairs. "Safety check."

Nico darted past Opal, getting the jump on her as he joined Tyler on the steps. Single-file, they descended after Emma. At the bottom, a diffuse glow illuminated a chamber half the size of the room above.

"Where's that light coming from?" Opal asked. Nico shrugged.

"Are we *underwater* right now?" Tyler's foot was tapping out of control.

"We must be," Opal replied. "The ceiling's ten feet above our heads."

There was no more arguing about who should be there. Not here, in a place where it felt like none of them should be.

Opal spotted a shadow in the room's center. A circle of black in the floorboards.

Emma aimed her light. They all moved close, stopping shoulder to shoulder at its edge.

"It looks like . . . water," Tyler whispered.

"Like a well," Nico murmured. "Or pool."

In a hole in the bottom of the houseboat, black liquid spun slowly, as if stirred by unseen hands. The inky water rolled against a low wooden lip built around the opening, but it never flowed into the room.

The pool simply . . . swirled. Ceaselessly. Relentlessly.

A million questions turned in Opal's mind. Was this part of the pond? The cove? Why did the water swirl? What kept it from surging out and flooding the chamber? Was it even water at all?

She knew only two things for certain.

The pool was the darkest thing she'd ever seen.

And it went deep.

7

NICO

*N*one of these came out," Emma grumbled, chomping on a Dorito.

She shoved her phone toward Nico across the cafeteria table. He squinted down at the photos. It was true—all of the shots Emma had taken of the pool were blurry. It was like the water didn't want its picture taken, though Nico knew that was crazy.

How crazy? You felt that thing. Not as much as Opal, but still.

They'd stood above the hole in silence, marveling at the whirling black liquid. Then Opal had jerked around and hurried up the stairs. Tyler was behind her in a blink, and suddenly Nico hadn't wanted to be down there, either.

Only Emma resisted, snapping a series of shots before reluctantly following the others. Climbing the steps, Nico had felt eyes on his back that didn't belong to his friend, something he knew was impossible but was equally impossible to shake.

Opal had gone straight through the showroom and foyer, bolting out the front door and across the stepping-stones. Only when completely off the pond did she stop, hands on her knees, a sheen of sweat dampening her forehead.

It would've been comical if Nico hadn't felt the same way. A weird sort of panic had gripped him, down there in the dark. He'd felt . . . small. Vulnerable. Like a rabbit sensing a cat, and knowing it had strayed too far from its hole.

"The light was bad," Tyler said, fidgeting with his ear. "That must explain the pictures. I wonder how far down that well goes."

"Deep," Emma said solemnly. "And dark. That's what Opal kept saying, when she was trying to calm down. Dark, deep, dark, deep. Over and over."

An icy spider walked up Nico's neck. He'd heard Opal, too.

"It was cold in there." Nico shivered at the memory. "Plus, I can't figure out that lower level at all. Houseboats usually have a flat underside, with almost no draft. Who'd build a ship with that much of it jutting underwater? It's like an iceberg. You could never move the thing."

"Who parks a dilapidated funhouse boat on a creepy pond in the middle of a deserted island?" Tyler spread his hands. "The whole thing is crazy. I think we should leave it alone."

Emma shook her head, her focus turned inward. "I think the houseboat is there because of the Darkdeep beneath it. That *must* be why. Nothing else fits."

Tyler covered his eyes and groaned. "Tell me you didn't give it a name. Now we'll never get away from it."

Emma's brow crinkled in disbelief. "Get away from it? You're joking, right? We just found, like, *the coolest thing in the world*, and you wanna pretend it's not there? Aren't you *insanely* curious about that pool? Did you notice the water never stopped moving?"

"Of course I noticed!" Tyler slumped in his chair, his head flopping back to stare at the ceiling. "Gave me the willies, too. That's all I dreamed about last night, except that the pool—"

"The Darkdeep," Emma said.

"—was inside my toilet bowl, and I was out of other options." His face scrunched at the memory. "I woke up sweating like a shoplifter."

"Whatever that well"—Nico held up a hand to forestall Emma—"that *Darkdeep* is, I get the feeling it's been there a long time. Like, maybe forever."

"Why does it swirl?" Tyler intoned slowly, squeezing his forehead. "I can't get over that part."

Nico grimaced. "Maybe there's a crack at the bottom of the pond. That might explain a whirlpool—it could just be freshwater spilling into the cove."

Tyler nodded uncertainly. Emma gave Nico a skeptical look. "Did you notice the strange way it was spinning, though?" she said. "Like in slow motion, almost. It didn't seem fast enough to be a whirlpool."

"Maybe the cove's salt water balances it out," Nico said defensively. He didn't have a good answer but was determined to believe one existed. Otherwise his mind crept to conclusions that scared him.

"We need to find out everything we can about the Darkdeep," Emma insisted, tapping the table with an index finger. "Someone's *got* to know about it. Maybe try the library?"

Tyler snorted, taking a pull off his milk before responding. "You think Old Lady Johnson has a book called *The Secret Houseboats of Still Cove*?"

Nico chuckled. "I gotta agree with Tyler. That showroom was buried under a foot of dust. It's been years since anyone set foot inside. And rumors would be all over Timbers if anyone had ever seen it before."

"We should still *look*." Emma began chewing on her curly blond hair. "The houseboat had to come from somewhere. What if it's listed in a shipping registry? Or maybe some logbook by whoever built it."

Nico nodded, biting into a carrot stick. "Okay, you're right. It can't hurt to try."

"Ah, man." Tyler shook his head. "You fold so easily, Holland. Like a deck of cards. Like a folding chair."

"She's right, though. *Someone* gathered all that stuff out there. Wouldn't you like to know who? And why?"

Tyler sighed dramatically, but nodded.

Emma opened her mouth. Closed it. Opened it again. "I think we should include Opal."

Nico's head snapped up. "No way."

Emma lifted a palm. "Just hear me out."

"I *told* you he'd say no," Tyler mumbled in a singsong voice.

Emma shot a glare at Tyler, then refocused on Nico. "Like it or not, Opal has a point. She *was* there when we found the houseboat, so she *does* have as much right to explore it as we do. But think about it this way—what happens if she gets mad we won't share, and decides to bring other people so she's not alone?"

Nico felt a chill cut through him. He knew which people Emma was talking about.

A memory flashed in his head—Opal, hunched over and gripping her knees after fleeing the houseboat. Her meltdown had only lasted moments, but Nico was sure she'd experienced something down there in the dark, beside the endlessly spinning pool.

Would she even want to go back? Did *he*?

"I still can't figure how she got onto the island," Tyler mused.

Nico frowned. He had no idea either, and Opal had refused to tell. *Smugly.*

"I'm just saying, think about it." Emma lowered her voice. "I don't think Opal means to be a jerk. I know she feels bad for . . . about that day."

The sympathy he'd felt evaporated in a blink. The image of his drone vanishing into the fog still riled Nico every time. "I'll think about it," was all he managed.

"Good." Emma sat back. "By the way, did you hear what the town is planning?"

Nico shook his head, thrown by the change in topic.

"A freaking *radish* festival." Emma giggled. "To boost tourism."

"A what?" Nico cringed. "Why?" Tyler just blinked in confusion.

"It's the official vegetable of Timbers," Emma said in a mock-scolding tone. "Remember? We learned that in second grade. Because of all the radish farms outside of town."

"But a radish festival?" Tyler ran a hand over his face. "Oh boy, that's bad."

"Uh-huh," Emma agreed. "And it's a big deal. There's gonna be a pageant, a parade, and lots of things on Main Street. All about radishes. It sounds totally ridiculous."

"Hey, show some respect," Nico joked. "You can't make radish tacos without radishes."

Tyler snorted, but then his gaze flicked to the door. A four-letter word escaped his lips. Nico turned. Logan was walking toward him with a vicious twinkle in his eye.

Jeez. Not again.

"Hey, flyboy!" Logan stopped directly behind Nico and loomed over him, talking loud enough for every table to hear. "Have you packed yet?"

Nico's eyebrows rose. Whatever this was, it wasn't what he'd expected.

"Packed?"

"For your move," Logan said matter-of-factly. Then he leaned over and mock-whispered in Nico's ear. "Or maybe you don't know?"

Nico spun awkwardly so he could stand and face Logan. Tyler scowled across the table. Emma had a white-knuckle grip on her tray.

"Say what you came to say," Nico muttered, resigned to another public humiliation.

Logan made a sad face, but he couldn't keep the glee from his voice. "I just want to wish you luck, wherever your family ends up. Getting transferred is rough, I know, but it's part of the ranger life, right, buddy? You'll do fine in Alaska, or wherever there are trees that need hugging."

Nico blinked, unable to process the taunt. "What are you talking about?"

Logan chortled. "Oh, wow. I guess I really do have to deliver the bad news." He clapped a hand on Nico. "My father made some calls last week. *Your* father isn't very popular around here, except maybe with owls. Everyone agrees he'd be better off in another park, somewhere far away from Timbers."

The blood drained from Nico's face. "That's . . . that's not . . ."

"Happy trails, I guess." Logan squeezed Nico's shoulder, acid coating his words. "Your dad shouldn't have messed with my family. Lesson learned, but too late for you. See ya." He turned and strode from the cafeteria, igniting a firestorm of whispers.

Nico's head spun. His knees felt weak. *Moving? From Timbers?* Emma and Tyler were on their feet, mouths working, but he couldn't hear them. Couldn't take any more. He had to get out of there. Everyone was staring at him.

Nico shoved his chair aside and ran from the building.

Fifteen minutes later, he was home. His father's beat-up old Range Rover was in the driveway, which relieved and terrified Nico at the same time. He found him in the kitchen eating a bagel. Bags of groceries littered the countertop.

Warren Holland looked up with a frown. "Nico? Why aren't you in school?"

"Is it true?" Nico blurted, red-faced and panting.

"Is what true?" his father replied, concern sharpening his features. "Why are you out of breath? Sit down. Are you hungry?"

Nico didn't move. "Is it *true*, Dad? Are you being transferred?"

"Who told you that?" His father's face became impassive. "*No*, Nico, I didn't get a transfer order this week. But I work for the government, son, and sometimes they need people in different locations. Department reviews are common, and this one isn't any different. It's not my place to question my bosses. Nor is it yours," he added pointedly.

"A review?" Nico felt something rip open inside of him. "But they're only doing it because Logan's dad asked them to!"

Warren Holland's voice grew icicles. "Sylvain Nantes has zero say in my employment. I work for the park service, period."

Nico wanted to scream. He wanted to break things and howl. "It's not fair! I have *friends* here, Dad. I don't want to move!"

His father stood, straightening to his full height of six feet six inches. His expression was stony. "Enough of this. You're a kid. It's not your job to worry about these things. I've done good work here, but I can do it elsewhere with my head held high if that's what my superiors decide. Now get back to school before you miss any classes. I'll expect you at dinnertime."

"But—"

"No buts." His dad pointed at the door. "Move it. Now."

Swallowing a thousand things he wanted to say, Nico stormed from the house.

8

OPAL

Here, Opal."

Kathryn Walsh pushed a bowl of fruit across her desk. "Have a snack."

Opal obediently took an apple. "Do you need me long, Mom? I have a *ton* of homework."

The text her mom had sent earlier said:

Come to the bank after school. We need to talk. NN.

"NN" meant "non-negotiable." Her mother used it way more than necessary, but Opal got in trouble if she ignored those letters.

"I want to discuss Citizen Radish," Kathryn said.

"Wha?" Opal asked, mid-chew. Her mother looked the same as always—blouse and skirt, gold earrings, lovely, clever face. But maybe the stress of managing Timbers Bank & Loan had finally gotten to her.

"There's going to be a pageant at the radish festival," her mother said. "Open to kids ages twelve to sixteen, looking for the best young leaders in Timbers. There will be a talent portion as well." She sounded like she'd memorized a press release.

Opal slumped in her seat. "That sounds *so* cheesy."

"It does *not*," her mother said sternly. "The pageant will be inclusive and intelligent, and there's no appearance component."

Opal didn't roll her eyes, but barely. "Awesome."

"It *is* awesome." The word sounded ridiculous when her mom used it. "Being crowned Citizen Radish will look outstanding on a college application."

Opal put down her apple. "Oh no."

"Oh yes." Her mother slid a paper across the desk. "This is your application. We'll go over it tonight when I get home."

Opal started to object but saw "NN" in her mother's eyes. She sighed. "Can I go now?"

Having gotten what she wanted, Kathryn Walsh smiled. "Of course. It looks like someone's waiting for you, anyway."

Opal turned. Logan was standing at the teller's counter with a free lollipop, the kind you were only supposed to get by making a deposit. *Ugh.* She'd been avoiding him as much as she could since the incident with Nico.

"Off you go!" her mother said. She *loved* the whole Nantes

family, because they kept so much money at the bank, lived in the best house on Overlook Row, and threw a swanky holiday party every year. Opal strode from her mother's office and headed straight for the front door.

She had one foot on the sidewalk when Logan stuck his head outside. "Opal!" he called, flashing a tentative smile. She kept walking.

"Wait a sec." Logan hurried to catch up. "Hey, why are you acting like a jerk?"

Opal spun, hot words ready. "*I'm* the jerk? You made Nico fall into Still Cove!"

"Huh?" Logan squinted at her. "What are you talking about? I flew his stupid toy into the fog."

Opal winced. She'd forgotten—Logan didn't know about Nico's fall, and Nico *definitely* wouldn't want him to.

"That *stupid toy* cost all his savings," Opal shot back, hoping Logan wouldn't catch her slip-up. She stormed off again, but Logan matched her pace.

"What do you care? Got a crush on him or something?" Logan's jawline hardened, his voice low and mean. "He's a total loser."

"He is not."

"He's moving, anyway. Didn't you hear? His dad's getting transferred."

Opal stopped. "What? Who told you that?"

They were standing in front of Brophy's Grocery, with its

country market vibe and hand-lettered displays. A giant CELE-BRATE THE RADISH FESTIVAL banner filled the window.

"My father." Logan couldn't fight back a grin. "He's probably arranging it."

A trapdoor opened in Opal's gut. "He can't do that."

"Oh, you'd be surprised."

Logan's back was to the store, but Opal could see people inside. *Just what I need*. Her mom would flip if she made a public scene.

Opal smiled wide and fake for their audience. "You really can be a total jerk, Logan. Goodbye."

She walked away without looking back.

―――――――

Nico pushed through the velvet curtain. "Next time you're late, we're leaving without you, Opal." He'd ignored her completely until now, not saying a word as they paddled across Still Cove.

"Sorry," Opal said. "My mom wanted to talk."

"How'd you get here yesterday?" Emma's tone was light, but Opal could tell she was dying to know.

"I used my teleporter," Opal said breezily. She hid a smile as the others exchanged glances. They had their secrets. It was fair to have one of her own. "So, what's on the agenda for today?"

Nico walked to the far corner of the showroom. "Emma,

Tyler, and I are exploring the collection. You can do whatever you want."

"I'm starting an inventory." Tyler fished a pencil from the pocket of his jeans and aimed it at a leather-bound book. "A catalog of everything on the boat. Wanna help?"

Nico shot him an annoyed glance.

"Okay!" Opal agreed cheerfully, pretending not to notice Nico's irritation. *It'll drive him nuts if me and Tyler start getting along.* Plus, anything was better than visiting the pool again. Although . . . she kind of wanted to.

"Excellent." Tyler rubbed his hands together like a cartoon villain. "Nico? Emma?"

"Fine," Nico grunted, kneeling to examine a wire birdcage in the corner.

"Sure thing, Ty." Emma cracked her knuckles. "For a while. But then the Darkdeep!"

Tyler flipped open the leather book with a flourish. "Behold . . . precious nothing!"

Opal giggled. "Is the whole thing blank?"

"Yeah." Tyler tapped the first page with his finger. "But look at these lines and columns. I'm pretty sure it's a logbook of some kind. Might as well use it for our records."

Nico joined them, his posture oozing reluctance. "Why do this now?"

"So we know what's here," Tyler said primly. "In order to appreciate it."

Opal agreed completely. If they understood the collection better, maybe they could figure out why it existed, or who put it together. She picked up a glass box containing a claw of some kind. "Start with this?"

"Why not?" Tyler's eyes danced. "We'll sort everything into categories, and then make *sub*categories . . ."

"You're *killing* me, Ty." But Nico lifted a battered wicker basket and peeked inside.

"Go ahead, Opal." Tyler licked the tip of his pencil. "What should I write down?"

"It's a black talon. Petrified. Likely from a bird. That's all I got."

"Great. Put it in the cabinet behind you. We'll label that *Shelf 1A*." He pulled a stack of Post-its from his pocket. The dude was a walking supply store. "Talk to me, Nico. Whatcha got?"

"It's best described as a fossilized turd."

"Gross." Opal wrinkled her nose. "Don't be revolting."

"No." Nico held up a hardened brown lump. "I really think it is."

"Yikes." Tyler made a gagging sound. "Just put that back where you found it."

"Put it in the pond." Opal looked to Emma for commiseration, but she was nowhere in sight. "Where'd Emma go?"

"Probably downstairs." Tyler lifted a stuffed . . . something off the floor. "She's obsessed with the pool. Calls it the Darkdeep."

The Darkdeep. The name raised goosebumps along Opal's arms. "Shouldn't someone go with her? Safety in numbers, and all that?"

"Emma's fine," Nico snapped. "She's not stupid. None of us are."

Opal turned away. She knew they weren't stupid. Nico was being such a jerk. And she really didn't think anyone should be down by the pool alone. She walked toward the stairs, passing a row of old photographs on the wall, and paused. The pictures had been taken over different eras, and hung in mismatched frames, but they all had something in common.

At first she thought it was their eyes. The oldest photos had that old-timey-stare thing going, but something was strange about the newer ones, too. Then it hit her: The people weren't looking at the camera. Or at anything, maybe. They were staring into space. Almost like they looked . . . beyond. It was true in every picture, even though the photos clearly spanned decades. Opal found it unnerving.

And that wasn't all. Each subject wore a carved necklace with a swirly design.

"Are you checking on Emma or not?" Nico yelled across the room, startling her.

Shaking her head, Opal walked to the top of the staircase. "Emma?"

"Down here!" she replied cheerily.

Opal swallowed and started down, gripping the railing tight. Emma began chattering the second she reached the bottom. "I think this is regular freshwater," Emma said, "or close to it. I snagged some pH strips from Mr. Huang's classroom and ran a test."

Opal looked at her in surprise. "Um, okay."

Emma was kneeling beside the pool. She waved a hand above the inky water. "There's no reflection, which is super weird, because there *is* light down here. I can't tell where it comes from. And this liquid shines anyway. *But it doesn't reflect.* What's *that* about?"

"Don't touch it." Opal warned. Her skin tingled with something like static electricity.

"What in the *world* makes it spin?" Emma chewed her thumbnail. Then she swung her legs around from under her and took off a shoe and sock.

Opal went cold. "What are you doing?"

Emma didn't answer. She extended a bare foot out over the swirling water.

"Emma, *no.*" Opal edged forward. "Stop. We don't know what that is."

"I just want to check something. If the surface feels . . ."

Emma dipped in her big toe.

The water went still.

Opal felt a charge pass through her body. "Emma, get ba—"

The Darkdeep rippled, as if a stone had been dropped into its heart.

Black liquid surged over the lip and encircled Emma's ankle. She was yanked down into the pool, disappearing slippery-quick and without a sound.

The water stilled, then resumed churning, twice as fast.

Opal stared at the empty space where the other girl had been.

And screamed.

PART TWO
FIGMENTS

9

NICO

A shriek echoed up the spiral steps.

Nico froze, a silver seahorse figurine locked between his fingers. Tyler stiffened behind the logbook. When the scream ripped through the boat a second time, they both ran for the staircase, Tyler shaking like a dog coming in out of the snow.

No no no no was all Nico could think as he tore down the stairs.

Opal was staring into the Darkdeep. Heavy tears streaked down her face.

"Where's Emma?" Nico demanded.

"In . . . in there!" Opal stammered, pointing to the pool's swirling mouth. "She barely touched it, but . . . I couldn't . . . Nico, it *dragged* her down!"

Nico's pulse pounded. The water was rotating faster than before. He peered into the pitch-black depths. He still couldn't see a thing, but was it gleaming more brightly? Ignoring the danger, he knelt close, desperate for any sign of his friend.

"I told her to be careful!" Tyler began circling the pool, his fists pressed to his temples. "Oh, man. Oh no!"

Nico glared at Opal, anger and fear making his voice harsh. "What happened?"

Opal blinked, chest heaving. "It wasn't my fault!"

Nico made a chopping motion with both hands. "Just tell me what happened!"

"Emma was testing the pool. She . . . she dipped her toe into the water."

Tyler kicked the lip of the well. "*I told her to be careful!*" His knobby shoulders began to shake.

"Okay." Nico squeezed his forehead, trying to think. "The water has to go somewhere. So maybe she . . . she might be able to—"

"To *what*?" Tyler shouted. "That thing pulls straight down! There's nowhere for Emma to go. She's gone, and it's our fault!"

Nico began stuttering a reply, but Opal clamped a hand on his forearm. "Nico, she didn't fall. The Darkdeep *pulled* her in. What *is* this thing?"

Tyler yanked off his hoodie. "I'm going after her."

"Are you crazy?" Nico shouted, even as Opal yelled, "Do *not* touch that water!"

Tyler threw his sweatshirt to the ground. "We have to do something!"

Nico couldn't form a coherent thought. "A rope?" he

suggested weakly. "Maybe she's stuck below the boat or something?"

"She won't see a rope in *that*," Tyler moaned, waving a hand at the Darkdeep. His voice dropped to a childlike whisper. "What should we do, Nico? She . . . it's been too long."

Nico was shaking his head miserably, out of ideas, when another cry shattered the quiet. His eyes shot to the staircase. This sound had come from above.

"Emma!" Tyler charged back up the stairs, screaming her name at the top of his lungs.

Opal hurried after him. Nico followed with his heart in his throat, hoping for a miracle.

Outside, the chill hit Nico like a hammer blow. The island felt twenty degrees colder than before, and the mist was twice as thick. Nico spotted a crumpled form at the edge of the pond. Tyler was racing on an intercept course.

"Let's go, Opal," Nico said, but the words were unnecessary. Opal shot across the entry stones like she'd been released from a bowstring. It was all Nico could do to keep up.

Tyler reached Emma and slid down beside her. By the time Nico and Opal arrived, he'd rolled her over and she was coughing wetly. Nico nearly fainted with relief.

Emma gagged and puked, unloading a bucket of pond water from her stomach.

But she was breathing. She was alive.

Tyler babbled with joy, hugging Emma so hard she was

struggling to catch her breath. Opal gently untangled Tyler's grip and sat Emma up. Nico stood a pace away, mouthing silent prayers of thanks to every deity that might be listening.

"Holy crap," Emma wheezed. "Wow."

Opal stroked Emma's sopping blond hair, trying to calm her down. She was shaking from way more than the cold. "What happened?" Opal whispered. "How'd you end up out here?"

"I w-wanted to see what it f-f-felt like," Emma spluttered. "But w-when m-my . . . when I t-t-touched it . . ." She shuddered from head to foot. "Some . . . *power* l-l-latched on to m-me. Like, a f-force or something. Next thing, I was d-dragged straight down, and it was all colors and lights, and I c-c-couldn't b-breathe."

Tyler glanced at Nico, eyes worried. Nico shrugged helplessly where Emma couldn't see.

"Guys," Emma continued in a low voice, staring at the pond. "The Darkdeep isn't natural. I felt a . . . a presence down there. Like a spy inside my head."

The hairs on Nico's arms stood. He rubbed them, trying to shake off a sensation of being watched. "Emma, that water is super cold, and you were down a long time. It's a miracle you surfaced out here. You almost . . . the lack of oxygen must be what you felt."

Emma shook her head adamantly. "No. Nico, I'm telling you, there's more going on here than a freaky whirlpool."

"None of that matters right now." Tyler lurched to his feet. "It's freezing out here, and you're soaking wet. Let's go back inside. We can talk about this later."

Opal nodded quickly, and Nico agreed. Emma had nearly drowned. They needed to get her warmed up as soon as possible. They weren't avoiding the topic because it was frightening. Of course not. Not at all.

Emma staggered to her feet, but her gaze kept drifting to the water. Horror lurked in her eyes, but something else as well. Wonder? Fascination?

Tyler led the group, while Opal held Emma's hand. Nico came last, feeling guilty. Out of all of them, he'd done the least to help. He'd been useless right when his friends needed him most. *Like usual.*

Nico was working himself into a serious funk when the bushes beside him rustled. He glanced to his left. *Something* stared back. Nico stumbled backward in shock as a huge shape surged from the trees. It towered over him, grunting and snorting.

He heard the others stop, but no one made a sound.

Nico's brain finally accepted what he was seeing.

A giant purple grizzly bear was watching him with sharp eyes.

10

OPAL

Stand your ground, Nico! You can't outrun a bear!

Opal watched as the enormous creature loomed over him, sniffing the air suspiciously. Sunlight and clouds dappled shadows across its purple fur. It was terrifying. And magnificent. *Why is it so big? Why is it purple?*

Nico had his head down and was staring at the grass.

That's right, Opal thought. *Don't make eye contact.*

The bear lowered its head and growled. Nico trembled, but didn't move.

Opal's gaze flicked to the others. Tyler had frozen in place. Good. He knew the bear rules, too. But Emma's fingers twitched against her side. To Opal's horror, Emma stepped toward the bear.

The animal rumbled. And . . . shimmered. With a shock Opal realized she could see right through the creature, almost like a hologram. The bear turned to face Emma, a deep, low snarl rattling its throat. The sound vibrated through Opal like an earthquake.

"Emma," Opal whispered. "*Don't.*"

"It's okay." Emma was staring at the bear in wonder. "Guys, I *know* him."

"What?" Tyler hissed from the side of his mouth. "Emma, did you bump your head?"

Opal forgot to breathe as the bear dropped to all fours and walked toward Emma.

"Stop!" Tyler waved his arms above his head. "Get away from her!" His voice cracked, but he screamed louder anyway. "GO AWAY!" The bear swung its head to look at him.

"No, no," Emma said. She kept her eyes locked on the impossible purple animal. "Hey, big guy. It's me. *Bear*, it's me!"

The bear continued to watch Tyler, who'd gone still again. Opal wondered what it would feel like to have those huge eyes focused on her. Terrifying? Or . . . exhilarating?

Emma reached out. The animal turned. To Opal's shock, it bowed its head.

"*Bear*," Emma breathed. Her fingers stretched, almost touching the sparkling lilac fur . . .

The bear vanished.

"No!" Emma's face fell as she stood with her fingers outstretched, dripping pond water on the grass where the bear had crouched an instant before.

"Um." Nico cleared his throat. "What was that?"

"Where'd he go?" Emma moaned in disappointment.

"There was a bear here just now." Tyler dropped to his knees. "A giant purple grizzly bear. I saw it."

Opal's legs felt like Jell-O. She put a hand on Tyler's shoulder, as much to steady herself as to comfort him.

"Where is it?" Nico peered into the forest. "Did you see it run off?"

"I *know* that bear," Emma repeated.

"Excuse me?" Nico and Opal spoke at the same time.

Tyler pressed his cheeks with both hands. "There was a shimmering see-through temporary bear growling in my face ten seconds ago. Is everybody getting that?"

"You don't understand." Emma turned to face them. "That was my imaginary friend, from when I was little! I used to draw him all the time. His name was Bear."

"Great name," Nico said in a shaky voice. "Did you also have a dog named Dog?"

Emma didn't seem to hear. "That *was* him. I don't know how he became real."

"*Not* real," Tyler insisted. "Disappearing childhood bears are not real."

Opal swallowed, staring at where the creature had been. "It was, though. We all saw it."

"Not possible," Tyler said stubbornly.

Opal arched a brow at him. "A spinning whirlpool swallowed Emma and spit her out in this pond. *None* of this seems possible. The boat, the basement, this island. So why not a purple bear?"

"One that came from inside Emma's head?" Nico said softly.

"Maybe we're dreaming," Tyler said. "Or it's just me. I'm having some kind of weird nightmare."

"This isn't a dream," Opal said. "I'm awake and I'm here, too. Want me to pinch you?"

"Emma needs to dry off and get warm," Nico said. "The real-or-not bear didn't change that. Do you have anything else to wear?"

"I left my sweater in the display room," Emma said. "And my other shoe is downstairs."

"Let's get them." Nico started toward the stepping-stones.

"Wait!" Tyler spread his arms. "Back to the boat? What if the bear's in there?"

"Tyler, it's gone," Opal said. "It didn't run off. We saw it vanish."

"It could *reappear*," Tyler said doggedly. "It showed up with no warning just now."

Nico stopped. "What do you think happened?"

"The Darkdeep happened." Emma's eyes flashed, daring anyone to challenge her. "The pool must've read my mind and made Bear appear somehow. That's the only answer that makes sense."

"Stop freaking me out," Tyler grumbled, scratching the

side of his head. "Pond water doesn't read people's minds." He laughed nervously, glancing around at the others. "Otherwise, we'd run away this second and never come back, right?"

Never come back. Opal didn't know if she could do that. The island was eerie and dangerous, but also fascinating. She'd never been so creeped out *or* felt so alive. *And if what Emma said is true . . .* "Were you thinking about Bear when you fell into the pool?" Opal asked.

"No." Emma shuddered. "I was just afraid. And also . . . maybe a little excited."

"Excited?"

A shaky smile crept onto Emma's face. "Because I was going to know. One way or the other, I'd learn what the Darkdeep is." She shrugged, as if surprised by her own feelings. "I think it *is* regular water, for the record. It felt and tasted like it, only a little more . . . slippery."

"Regular water?" Tyler reared back with a scowl. "Emma, it *pulled you in*. And please, wash out your mouth if you drank any. Who knows what could happen?"

"Lights, colors, and something inside your head." Nico spoke slowly, as if considering every word. "Is that what you remember, Emma?"

She nodded. Opal had to admit the last part didn't sound great.

Nico rubbed his chin. "That seems scary."

"It *was*." Emma's hands fluttered as she tried to explain. "You know how when you're reading a book, your eyes go back and forth across the page? Well, it felt like something was reading me. Like *I* was the book."

They were silent after that. Opal caught Nico and Tyler sharing a worried look.

"Okay, real talk." Tyler squeezed his nose. "We're definitely not going back in that boat right now. We should evacuate the island until we get a better handle on things."

"Leave?" Opal realized she didn't want to. "Why?"

"So that demon well doesn't eat the rest of us!" Tyler squawked.

"It didn't *eat* her. Emma touched the water on purpose."

"Emma's other shoe is on the houseboat," Nico pointed out.

"I don't need my shoe," Emma said, surprising Opal. "Tyler's right. Let's go home."

"Okay, sure." Nico kicked a pebble into the pond. Opal heard the reluctance in his voice.

He's as curious as I am.

Because Opal was practically *burning* with curiosity. What could make a purple bear spring into being? She wanted to examine the Darkdeep right away, but it was Emma who'd been sucked through a spin cycle and ejected into a freezing pond, just in time to meet her imaginary friend before it vanished into thin air. So, yeah. She got to make the call.

With nothing more to discuss, they climbed the ridge, heading for the rowboat. Opal wasn't ready to share her tunnel yet. Not until she was sure they'd keep including her. On the beach she and Nico each picked up an oar. They pushed off, the island disappearing behind them in the mists.

Nico cleared his throat. "Emma," he said quietly, rowing in sync with Opal. "You think you *made* that bear? That it somehow came from your imagination?"

"Yes." Emma spoke with absolute certainty. "It happened inside the Darkdeep."

More strokes. More silence. Finally, Opal cracked.

"I wonder if the rest of us could do it."

"Do what?" Tyler glanced from face to face. "Oh no. Don't tell me you're thinking about going in on purpose. Because there's nuts, and then there's *nuts*."

Nico kept rowing, his face an unreadable mask. Emma nodded as if Opal had made the logical conclusion.

Lay out all the cards.

"If I went into the Darkdeep," Opal said, "maybe *my* imaginary friends would appear."

"You can't be serious," Tyler said. "Go in? Into the black, sucking, mind-reading well?"

Opal shrugged. "Are you seriously *not* thinking about it?"

Tyler looked away. Nico grunted, dipping his oar in time with hers. Emma grinned.

As they slid toward the sheer cliff wall, Opal had only one thought.

What would the Darkdeep pull from her?

11

NICO

The chin strap fit snugly under Nico's neck.

He stared into the mirror, a feeling of intense humiliation spreading from his face, down his neck, to his limbs, fingers, toes, and the rest of his body.

I look like a royal dork.

"Hmmm." Warren Holland scratched at his beard, as close to a laugh as he ever got these days. It didn't improve Nico's mood.

"Dad, there's no way I'm wearing this," Nico pleaded, praying his father would save him from the town's idea of cutesy festival regalia.

"If the school sent it home, you have to wear it," Warren said sternly, his giant frame nearly filling Nico's bedroom. "Town pride is important, son. This festival is . . . um . . . Timbers is really trying to do something special."

Nico was dressed in a giant radish suit. A red, formless

blob of a body—stitched together by Ms. Simanson's sixth-period home economics class—matched to a green, beret-style cap with a jaunty leaf-and-stem combo on top. *Nightmare.*

Twenty of these monstrosities had been issued to random seventh graders for the parade, and Nico's luck remained reliably awful. Carson and Parker had laughed him out of school.

"You look *rad*." His father coughed into a fist. Did his lip twitch? Was he making a *joke*?

"Dad," Nico tried again, "this kind of thing will get me beat up. I can't—"

"No one is above supporting the community," his father interrupted, heavy brows knitting together. "People are counting on this to give the town a boost. Maybe restore some of the spirit we've lost since . . ."

Warren waved an absent hand. Nico didn't finish the thought, either. He knew his father had no regrets about saving the owls, and Nico didn't want to ask if he understood how much of the town's troubles were blamed on them. He worried his dad didn't care.

Warren Holland disappeared down the hallway. Nico ripped off the cap and threw it onto his bed, then wriggled out of the bell-shaped body. Maybe he could leave the costume outside, and bears might get it. No one could blame him then.

The thought took him back to Still Cove, and the impossible things that had happened. Nico had spent all of last night rationalizing away what he'd seen, then all morning pretending everything was normal.

He'd gotten through his early classes by keeping his head down, but when facing Emma and Tyler across the lunch table, he could no longer fool himself. Emma had fallen into the Darkdeep, and somehow a *purple freaking grizzly bear* sprang into existence as a result.

Emma seemed totally fine. She wasn't sick, or scared, or falling to pieces. If anything, she seemed energized. She wanted to go back to the island the second they could shake free of their parents, and Nico had agreed without a fight. He felt the same. They'd found something amazing that no one else knew about. How could they not explore it?

You don't know what it is, or what it can do.

Nico shrugged off the nagging doubt. He refused to be afraid this time. He didn't want everything about his life to be ordinary. This was special, and it was his, and he wasn't going to squander it.

They were meeting again in a half hour.

Tyler had promised to tell Opal, and Nico held his tongue. Even he accepted there was no way to keep her from something this big. Being honest, Nico wanted Opal there, too. If nothing else, she was smart and brave. She could help them figure out the Darkdeep.

The Darkdeep.

It was incredible. Maybe even magical. His skin tingled just thinking about it. The more he considered the houseboat, the more he believed it had been built to hide what swirled beneath it. The showroom was amazing—a collection of the coolest stuff imaginable—but the pool in the basement blew everything else away.

Impatience at maximum, Nico tugged on a navy pull-over and jeans and stepped into his sneakers, shoving a pair of trunks and an old towel into his backpack. *Would he really dare?*

He slung the backpack over his shoulder before he could psych himself out. The bike ride would take twenty minutes. He could get there early and explore the cave before the others arrived. He'd never really looked around in there. Maybe he'd missed something cool.

He tried to slip out the front door, but a squeaky floor-board gave him away.

"Nico!" his father called from the kitchen. "Hold on a sec, son. Come in here."

Nico squeezed his eyes shut, then snapped them open. He walked to the back of the house, bracing himself to lie how-ever much was necessary in order to escape.

His father was in his usual spot at the table. He kicked out the chair across from him.

"Sit. We need to talk."

Dread leached into Nico's chest. "Yeah?"

His father set down his coffee mug. "I was going to wait until your brother was back, but I know you've been wor-ried, and I don't want you hearing any rumors that might set you off."

Bad start. Bad, bad start.

"What kind of rumors?"

Warren Holland sighed, one arm reaching back to scratch between his shoulder blades. He wore his tan ranger uniform. His hat rested on the table. "I received a letter from the department today," he said. "Following the review, I've been selected for a non-disciplinary employment evaluation."

Nico shook his head in confusion. "What does that mean?"

"Nothing. At least, not by itself. These things happen all the time. Usually the department is assessing whether a ranger might be better suited for another position."

Nico's stomach dropped. "Are they firing you?"

"Of course not!" his father barked. "Maybe even the opposite. But a change in position often results in a transfer, so people don't have to work for their former coworkers. If my status were to change, I could be asked to move—"

Nico was up out of his chair so fast it fell over backward. He shot through the back door, ignoring his father's startled shout. Nico grabbed his bike and took off like he'd been fired from a cannon.

He heard the door fly open behind him. Nico put his head down and pedaled hard. He didn't stop until he'd bombed through downtown, blowing a stop sign on Main Street and drawing an aggrieved shout from Mr. Owens, who was busy taping radish streamers to the front of his barber shop.

Teeth clenched, Nico coasted up the steep climb of

Overlook Row, which stole the momentum from his tires and brought him to a stop. The famous houses marched in a line on his left. To his right, Orca Park rolled down to the waterfront.

Hot tears burned in his eyes, but he refused to cry. It was just so *unfair*. Nico hadn't done anything to anyone, yet he was being chased out of Timbers like a plague victim. Right as he discovered something astonishing. Right as his life threatened to become special.

Nico leaned across his handlebars to catch his breath. If he hadn't, he wouldn't have seen them.

As his face fell into shadow, Nico spotted two people in the park. Something about the posture of the smaller one caught his eye . . .

He rolled his bike closer. Squinted. Then he reared back in surprise.

Opal was sitting on a swing with her hands around the chains. Logan stood beside her, leaning against a pole. As Nico watched, they both laughed. A paper plate wrapped in cellophane sat on the ground between them.

"You've got to be kidding me," Nico whispered.

Anger flared in his gut. Was Opal just betraying *him*, or was she also spilling the secrets of the Darkdeep?

He'd been starting to trust her again. To like her, even. And there she was, hanging out with the sadistic bully whose family was getting his father transferred out of town.

Nico backed up slowly, so they wouldn't see. Then he rode away, jumping a curb into the rolling fields that stretched toward Still Cove.

He didn't say a word to Opal.

And if he never saw her again, that was fine too.

12
OPAL

Incoming figment at twelve o'clock."

Tyler's voice crackled through the walkie-talkie. From where Opal stood beside the pond, she could barely make him out on the sloped houseboat roof.

"What is it?" Opal asked.

"It's a . . . dinosaur." Tyler's voice was an octave higher than usual.

"*What?*"

Tyler had the binoculars. His job was to spot whatever appeared after someone went into the Darkdeep. It always spit the diver out into the pond, but the well's creations could materialize anywhere on the island.

Figments.

Nico had said it first, and the name stuck. Opal thought it was the perfect way to describe the things that escaped from their minds. Imaginings that were real, but also weren't.

They'd all changed into their swimsuits when they reached the houseboat—even Tyler, though it didn't stop him from grumbling about how crazy they were. But the issue was decided. They *were* going to test the pool. No matter how reckless it might be, Opal wanted to see what the Darkdeep might pull from her.

"Tyler, don't joke." Opal looked at Nico, who was wading out of the water, dripping and sputtering.

"I'm serious." Tyler snorted. "But it's not . . . well, you'll see."

"Where is it?"

"Right behind you."

Opal spun to face the woods.

Out stomped a six-foot orange T-Rex with teeth made of foam rubber and shiny brown eyes. It bumbled onto the grass and began to dance, swinging its arms and grinning.

Nico stopped dead. "Oh, crap."

"Pippo the Dinosaur?" Opal laughed, and she could hear Tyler cracking up over the walkie-talkie. "Nico, why were you thinking about him?"

"Shut up. It's not like I *tried* to." He turned his back on her. He'd been rude again all afternoon, and Opal had no idea why.

Pippo waddled over to Emma, who'd run to join them and was smiling like a loon in her Timbers swim-team suit. She tried to pat the dinosaur's back, but her hand passed right through it. Still, Pippo looked more solid than the last creation—a sparkling unicorn Opal had conjured. The figments lasted for only a few minutes before disappearing without a trace.

Pippo looked just like he did on his TV show. He tottered around, waving gleefully, but then spotted Nico.

Nico swallowed. His face was pale.

"Nico?" Emma asked. "Is something wrong?"

Out of nowhere, Pippo produced a giant bottle of Brack & Brack's No-Tangles Shampoo.

"No way." Nico looked more resigned than afraid. Pippo advanced, waving the bottle like an orchestra conductor. Nico backed up a step. "Stop it. I'm not five anymore. I'm not afraid of you."

Pippo cocked his head. He put the bottle down and stretched out his short T-Rex arms.

Nico shot a glance at Opal and Emma. Emma was smiling, but not in a mean way. Opal knew her own grin might be a *little* mean.

"Go ahead," Emma urged. "Try to hug him!"

Nico shook his head. A second later Pippo faded in a shimmering orange haze.

"I feel like we witnessed something special," Tyler wheezed, out of breath. He'd climbed down from the roof and sprinted over to join them, a soggy blue towel draped over his shoulders. "Nico, facing the dino-terror of his past. And nearly messing himself."

"I used to dream about Pippo." Nico blinked with distaste. "He'd appear in my bathroom and force-shampoo my hair. It . . . wasn't good."

"The two things you hated most." Tyler put a consoling hand on Nico's shoulder. "Pipposaurus Rex and daily personal hygiene. Not much has changed."

Nico shoved Tyler playfully. "Thanks a lot."

"Why'd you imagine Pippo if you don't like him?" Emma asked, stealing Tyler's towel.

"I didn't. He must've been lurking in my mind somewhere, and the Darkdeep picked him up. I'm not as good at this as you."

Emma had gone in more than anyone, racing back to the whirlpool as soon as her latest figment disappeared. She'd conjured up a Porg from *Star Wars*, Moaning Myrtle, and an Angry Bird perched on a seven-foot Pikachu.

"Hey, the mini-dragon you called up earlier was super cool." Emma frowned down at her phone. "I just wish we could take videos of these things."

Nico's dragon *had* been cool, Opal thought. They'd been going in one at a time to appreciate one another's creations. Tyler had agreed to make *one* dive, conjuring his favorite cartoon genius, Suzie Robotonic. After watching the mad scientist draft schematics on her magic whiteboard, he'd declared himself satisfied, and spent the rest of the time on the roof.

"Who's next?" Emma asked, bouncing on her feet.

"I'm good for now." Opal was still recovering from seeing

her idol, Sailor Jupiter, stalking through the trees. Though amazed by the figments, she found the Darkdeep unsettling— the way it touched her mind and filtered her imagination. Plus, she always came out spitting pond water. She needed more recovery time than Emma did.

Emma grinned. "Nico? Tyler?"

"You go ahead," Nico said. "We all know you want to."

"*Well*, if you insist!" She sprinted for the houseboat.

"I better get back to my post." Tyler whistled as he strolled toward the stepping-stones. Opal couldn't tell if he was afraid of the Darkdeep or was just being cautious, though it didn't dampen his mood. Tyler just didn't seem to want to go in again.

She did. Opal realized she was happy. Exhilarated. More and more she felt like part of the group, despite Nico's surliness. *Inside* the circle. Something new and wonderful was happening, and she was at the center of it.

Or something has awakened, and you're the cause.

Opal stopped short. Where did *that* notion come from?

The pond spewed Emma onto the shore, and she crawled out, coughing and shivering. It was getting late and the temperature had dropped.

"We should probably go soon," Opal said.

Nico didn't bother to respond.

Emma's teeth chattered. "That c-c-can be the l-last one."

"What'd you think about?" Opal asked. Emma was the

best at being intentional—her plunges usually resulted in figments she'd deliberately tried to imagine.

"Godzilla," Emma said simply.

Nico covered his eyes. "Oh, jeez."

Emma beamed. "Pippo gave me the idea."

"Great."

Suddenly, a shadow engulfed the group.

They all looked up. And up, and up, and up.

Godzilla.

Huge and reptilian, he towered above them.

"Emma, no," Opal breathed.

"It's fine." Emma sighed. "Bummer, though. He's only a fifth of his real size."

I wonder if he knows Pippo, Opal thought, backing away as the giant reptile took a step closer. He opened his mouth and roared, the sound fierce and full. A beam of blinding light shot from between his jaws.

"Wow," Emma whispered. "Hi."

Godzilla bellowed once more. Then, like a candle, he flickered and went out.

"*Aw*. He didn't last long," Emma said sadly. "I'm getting worse at this."

"Small Godzilla or not, that was by far the biggest figment yet." Nico stared at where the monster had been. "Maybe that's why he vanished so quickly."

Emma smiled, pleased. "Let's go dry off. I'm gonna make

a list of what I want to create tomorrow." Nico grinned, and they started toward the stones.

Opal was about to follow, but something caught her eye.

"You coming, Opal?" Emma called.

"Be right there! I want to check something."

As the others moved away, Opal walked across the field. *There*. She wasn't imagining it. On the ground where Godzilla had briefly stood was a slight indentation, the barest pressing of the grass. Opal took a deep breath.

She was looking at an enormous reptilian footprint.

13

NICO

Nico followed Emma and Tyler into the display room.

His temper had been slipping all day, but he didn't want to ruin their excitement. He'd tell them about Opal and Logan later, when they could put their heads together privately, and figure out a plan to keep her away for good.

Emma skipped down the center aisle. "What should we catalog next?"

Nico forced a smile. "You choose."

"Hmmm." Emma tapped a finger to her lips. "So many options." She pointed near the entrance to the Darkdeep's spiral staircase. "Maybe that pirate sword over there?"

Nico glanced at the wall, but his attention was snagged by the green thing on its pedestal. He'd never given the jar much thought, but something about it now . . .

Nico walked over and peered inside. Where at first the blob had been a hazy, billowing mass—like mercury—it now seemed to have more definition. The glossy green ball had stretched somehow, becoming more oblong in shape, like a turtle shell made out of Silly Putty. If Nico squinted, he thought he could see the vague outline of a head.

Then he snorted. *Sure, buddy, the sludge ball grew a noggin.* Nico turned back to the aisle, but as he did, he felt a prickling sensation between his shoulder blades.

Nico turned around, eyes darting. For a moment, he'd had the unmistakable impression of being watched. Yet there was no one else, not even Opal. The sensation faded quickly. Nico almost laughed, but his heart wasn't in it. At times the collection really gave him the creeps. Who put all these weird things together? Why? And where was that person now?

"Guys?" Nico called out. "Does this look different to you?"

Tyler looked up from a roll of parchment. "The jar thing? Different how?"

Nico ran a hand through his damp hair. "I don't know. Just . . . changed."

Emma was at his side in a heartbeat. "You know, it *does* look more solid. Did you shake it or something?"

"I've barely looked at it until now," Nico admitted, chuckling nervously. "But I could swear it was just a swirling glob of goo earlier."

"You think it's growing?" Emma whispered, eyes shining as she examined the jar.

Nico held up a hand. "It's probably nothing. Maybe it

warmed up in here. Or got colder. Whatever. Forget I said anything."

The curtain swished and Opal walked into the room, her face pinched as if she were deep in thought. Nico muttered something under his breath.

"What is it with you?" Emma whispered, elbowing him in the side. "You've been like an angry cat around her all day."

Opal must've heard. "I wouldn't mind knowing either," she said drily, crossing her arms. "I thought we were past this, Nico."

Nico's face clouded. "I thought we could trust you. I was wrong."

Opal shot him a baffled look. "What are you talking about?"

"This afternoon. Orca Park. Tell these guys who you were huddled up with, whispering secrets."

"What?" Then recognition dawned in Opal's eyes. "Oh, Nico, it wasn't like that."

"Logan Nantes." Nico bit off the name. "Whose dad is busy getting mine transferred to Antarctica. But you had a good laugh with your pal from Overlook Lane."

Opal's hands rose. "Nico, I swear, you've got it wrong. I didn't even want to be there."

"Could've fooled me. I saw you two cracking up by the swings."

"No, tha—"

"I bet you told him about the island, didn't you?" Nico's voice dripped with accusation. "The houseboat, the Darkdeep, figments, *everything*. Whatever it took to score points with the cool crowd."

Opal stared, openmouthed. Emma had stopped moving. Tyler nervously bit his lip. Finally, Opal squeaked, "I would *never*."

Nico jabbed a finger at her. "Then how come you didn't mention your little chat?"

"Because I know how much you hate him!" Opal shot back. "Logan isn't as bad as you think, but I'd never reveal our secrets. Give me a *little* credit."

Nico's hands flew up. "You're defending him?!"

Opal winced. "Okay, he's been awful to you, I admit it. Logan can't let go of his father's stupid grudge. But he has another side, too. I wish he'd let more people see it."

Nico scoffed, but Opal raised a palm as if she were about to swear an oath. "I didn't tell him anything," she promised. "It was his mom's idea we go to the park, and I couldn't get out of it. I spent the whole time counting down the seconds until I could bail and come here."

"Then what were you two giggling about, huh? Who'll buy my house after I'm gone?"

"I was trying to throw him off our scent!" Opal took a deep breath, as if struggling to keep her voice level. "Logan is suspicious about where I've been lately. I'm usually around our block a lot, but suddenly I'm never there." Her face reddened. "So I made up something," she mumbled at the floorboards.

"Made what up?" Emma asked.

Opal rolled her eyes. "I said I've been practicing a dance solo for the festival. 'A Radish Emerges,' I called it. Like, you know . . . me sprouting from a seed into a vegetable."

Tyler barked a giddy laugh. "Oh man, I'd pay to see that one."

"*That's* what we were laughing about," Opal said, glaring at Nico. "I even told him that messing with your dad was wrong. He didn't like that, but I said it anyway."

She fell silent. Nico was staring at his shoes.

"I didn't say a single word about this place." A hint of pleading entered Opal's voice. "I wouldn't do that. Not to any of you."

Nico's head rose. He met Opal's eye. "You swear it?"

"I swear."

Nico held her gaze a moment longer. "Okay. I'm sorry. I worried maybe . . . I thought . . ." He released a pent-up breath. "It doesn't matter what I thought. I was wrong and I've been acting like a jerk. My bad."

Nico heard Emma exhale. Tyler wiped his palms on his jeans with a relieved whistle. Opal was still standing apart from the others, as if unsure the storm had passed.

"Come on," Nico said, managing a grin. "We've got work to do."

Opal smiled. "Yup. And I just discovered something important."

Nico arched an eyebrow. Emma and Tyler looked Opal's way as well.

"I think the figments are getting stronger."

"Well, *yeah*." Tyler seemed underwhelmed. "The last ones weren't as hazy as the purple bear. I guess the Darkdeep needed a few rounds to warm up."

"It's not just that," Opal said. "Godzilla left a footprint behind!"

Nico shook his head. "But they're just figments. Ideas lifted from our heads. They aren't real, Opal. You can wave an arm right through them."

Opal shrugged. "I checked the grass. It's bent in the shape of a giant lizard foot."

"Godzilla's a dinosaur, not a lizard," Emma corrected automatically. "At least, he was in the original movie. A theropod."

Tyler covered his face. "How is that relevant?"

"Just saying."

"What *matters* is," Opal continued, "these figments are more real than just flimsy images. And they might be getting realer."

Nico's eyes tightened. "This is bigger than we thought."

"*Better* than we thought," Emma crowed.

"Okay, this seals it." Tyler tugged on the back of his neck. "We can't let anyone else find out about the Darkdeep. It might be dangerous."

"We have to guard it," Opal said. "Keep the whole island secret."

"*Guardians*." Emma's eyes rounded. "Oh man, we're going to need a cool name. What about the Darkdeep Keepers? No, no! The Whirling Well Watchers! Triple Dubs for short?"

Nico ignored her. "So that's it, huh? We're responsible for it now. And everything inside this boat."

Opal nodded. "Just us four. Assuming we're done arguing about whether I'm allowed to be here or not?"

Nico chuckled sheepishly. "What would we do without you?"

He stuck out his hand, palm down. Opal blinked, then covered it with her own. Tyler slapped his on next, followed by Emma's two-handed grip over the top. The four of them stood there, linked, facing off in the center of the silent showroom.

Tyler shuffled his feet. "Should, like, one of us say something?"

Nico grinned. "Sure. Go ahead."

"I was hoping you would." He looked at Emma, but she shook her head, giggling.

Nico glanced at Opal. Her eyes were gleaming. *Is she crying?*

"Opal?" he asked. "You have anything?"

She sniffed once, then smiled brilliantly. "I think we covered it, right?"

They all dropped their hands, bursts of laughter echoing up to the dusty rafters.

14

OPAL

A cute ninth grader strode down the hall toward Opal.

Cute ninth grader Evan Martinez, to be exact. "Opal Walsh?" he said.

"Yup." *Why did I just say "yup"?!?* she chided herself, but also, he knew her name! She hitched her backpack higher. "Hi, Evan."

"Your mom's waiting in the front office. I'm supposed to come get you."

"Oh. Great."

She didn't know whether to be mad at her mom for dropping by the school, or pleased she got to walk with Evan Martinez. He was wearing his soccer uniform. She hoped everyone saw.

Ooh! Maybe Evan Martinez could show up as a figment one day.

No. Tyler and Nico would crush her for it. Emma might understand.

When they arrived at the office, Evan held the door for her. "Thanks," Opal said.

"No problem." He sat down behind the STUDENT AIDE placard. Opal had a sudden desire to apply to be a student aide.

"Opal!" Kathryn Walsh called. "Hello, sweetie."

"Hey, Mom." Opal tore her gaze from Evan, who was stapling papers in a very arresting way. "Everything okay?"

"Weren't you expecting me?" Kathryn opened the door for Opal and they walked out into the hall. "Today's the pageant orientation meeting. It's in the auditorium right now."

"I forgot." In fact, Opal hadn't read that part. Or any part. She'd just signed the document her mother put in front of her.

Once inside the auditorium, they sat in two plush theater seats. A decent number of seventh and eighth graders were there. Opal was surprised to see high schoolers, too—she'd assumed older kids would be able to get out of this.

Opal waved to Azra Alikhan from geography, who definitely had a chance to win. Azra could play piano and had cool glasses. Opal couldn't compete with that. She was just hoping not to come in last. *Is there a last? Jeez, I hope not.*

"Hello, Walshes! What a nice surprise. May we sit by you?"

Opal looked up to see Mrs. Nantes standing at the end of their aisle.

And Logan. What on earth?

"Of course!" Kathryn and Opal scooted over to make

room. "It's good to see you, Lori. Opal thanks you for the lovely treat yesterday, don't you, honey?"

Opal nodded dutifully. "Thanks, Mrs. Nantes."

Logan's mom smiled. "It was nothing. I'm glad you kids had fun."

Lori Nantes made amazing caramel-stuffed chocolate-chip cookies. It was those cookies that had trapped Opal with Logan in Orca Park the day before. He'd shown up on her porch with a plastic-wrapped plate and orders from his mother to share. Opal's mom had practically shoved her out the door.

Logan sat down beside Opal, staring straight ahead.

"Hi, Logan."

"Hey."

Opal fell silent, amazed he was there. She couldn't believe his mother was making him do this.

"Logan," her mother said. "I didn't know you were entering the pageant."

"It was his idea." Mrs. Nantes sounded vaguely shocked. "He filled out the application and everything."

Logan's ears burned red. He still wasn't looking at Opal.

"That's . . . wow." Opal fought down a grin. "What's your talent?"

"I'm going to dribble a basketball while I'm standing on my head."

"I'm not sure that's what the committee had in mind, but

it's . . . something." Mrs. Nantes' eyes widened in delight. "And I hear Opal is doing a dance!"

"A what?" Opal's mother twisted to look at her.

"She's been practicing all week." Logan didn't even try to hide his grin. "It's about being a radish. An *emerging* radish, right, Opal?"

Opal swallowed. "Yeah. About that."

"You're going to dance?" Kathryn Walsh sounded flummoxed. "I thought you were reciting one of Shakespeare's soliloquies."

Another part of the application Opal hadn't examined. Still, anything was better than dancing in front of the whole school.

Principal Kisner walked onstage and tapped the microphone. "Welcome to rehearsal," she intoned. "I'd like to introduce our radish festival chairman, Mr. Albert Murphy."

What? The grump who lived next to Nico? Why was *he* in charge?

"Sorry, Mom," Opal whispered. "I forgot. I'll do the Shakespeare thing instead."

"No, no." A light had kindled in her mother's eyes. "A dance will be *beautiful*. I always knew you loved dancing."

Crap. Crappity crap crap.

"Would all pageant participants please come forward?" Mr. Murphy said. "No need to be nervous. We're going to ask each of you a practice question, just to get the ball rolling."

Logan and Opal followed the crowd backstage behind a heavy blue curtain. It reminded her of the houseboat. She couldn't wait to get back. What figment would she create next? And Godzilla had left a *footprint*. What did that mean?

"I can't believe I volunteered for this," Logan muttered as they shuffled into the line.

"Why did you?" Opal asked. Logan hated public speaking. He hurried through school presentations so fast you could barely understand him. And he never signed up for anything except sports.

"I don't know," Logan grumbled miserably.

"There's still time to get away. You could sneak out through the drama room."

Logan locked eyes with her. "Would you come with me?"

Opal looked away, suddenly embarrassed. "I can't. My mom would chase me down. There's no way out for me." She'd tried to sound funny and dramatic, but Logan didn't laugh. The line began moving as other kids gave short, awkward answers to Mr. Murphy's questions.

Logan's jaw firmed. "Then I'm staying, too."

Opal wanted to ask why, but Logan spoke again, his words tumbling out. "I don't get you. We hung out together all summer, and I thought you had fun. But then this thing with Nico happened, and now you're totally avoiding me. Why?"

Opal tried to collect her thoughts. Had Logan entered the pageant because of her? That was insanity.

"If he'd let me buy him a new drone, I would," Logan went on. "But Nico wouldn't take it. He's too stubborn, just like his dad."

"You shouldn't have ruined his first one." And Opal remembered how scared she'd been after Nico fell. Logan didn't know the half of it.

Logan shifted uncomfortably. "I thought he'd find it."

"In Still Cove? Well, he didn't."

There were only two kids left in front of them. The stage lights made it so Opal couldn't see out into the auditorium, but she knew her mother was watching. "What do you see as the biggest challenge facing Timbers?" Mr. Murphy asked Megan Cook.

"Those owls?" Megan answered, her voice unsure. "Making them go away?"

"Look, I'm sorry," Logan whispered, "but Nico is still a loser. Why are you following him around? What are you guys doing? You're never home, and your mom didn't know anything about your 'emerging radish dance.'" He used air quotes.

Opal said nothing. Megan finished answering.

Logan narrowed his eyes. "Where do you go every day, Opal?"

Opal pushed past the next person in line and marched out to center stage.

Mr. Murphy regarded her coolly from behind his bifocals. "State your name, please."

"Opal Walsh."

"Opal, in your opinion, what is Timbers' greatest strength?"

A long pause. Opal was thinking about everything but the question.

Finally, Mr. Murphy cleared his throat.

"The people," Opal answered, speaking from a place she couldn't name. "Everyone cares about each other. That's important."

Opal stepped away and continued across the stage. She didn't look back at Logan, but it was *his* question that echoed inside her head.

Where do you go every day, Opal?

She worried Logan was determined to find out.

15

NICO

I'm telling you, she's overdoing it."

Tyler dipped his oar into Still Cove. "All afternoon, Emma cannonballs into the vortex, splashes out of the pond, checks her latest insane creation, and then sprints back to do it all over again. It's too much."

Nico stopped paddling long enough to scratch his nose. "How many times has she gone?"

"What, today?" Tyler shook his head. "I lost track after ten."

Nico whistled.

The mist parted and he could finally see the island ahead. Both boys jumped out to pull the boat onto the beach. Nico zipped his windbreaker as a polar gust swept the sand. He couldn't wait to get inside the houseboat and warm up.

"Thanks for getting me," Nico said. "Sorry I took so long. My dad held me up at home, and then Opal wasn't at the meeting spot like we'd planned. I guess she's not coming."

"No biggie." Tyler tossed his oar inside the rowboat. "Honestly, I wanted off the island for a while anyway."

Nico glanced at him, surprised. "Off? Why?"

Tyler rolled his eyes. "You'll see."

Something rattled the bushes nearby. A moment later, three tiny blue Smurfs burst from the trees. Nico's jaw dropped. "Right on cue," Tyler muttered.

The lead Smurf—a stout, bearded fellow—spotted them and pointed. To Nico's shock, he heard a squeaky voice yell, "*Attack!*" followed by two more high-pitched war cries. The Smurfs charged and began kicking sand onto Nico's shoes, snarling and shaking their little fists.

"Not again." Tyler shooed the pint-sized assailants. "Can you give it a rest, please?"

"*War! War!*" The leader began beating his chest, but a moment later the trio blipped out of existence. Nico and Tyler were alone again.

Tyler put a hand to his forehead. "*Finally.* Those guys have been driving me crazy."

Nico was staring at his feet. "Tyler. There's sand on my shoes."

"Mine too. Those little creeps showed up mad and never stopped."

"Tyler, those figments *moved the sand*. And they were talking to us."

"You think I don't know?" Tyler removed a sneaker and shook it out. "The new ones won't shut up. They last longer, too. I've been waiting for that crew to poof since they declared war on the 'pond giants,' or whatever they kept calling me."

Nico blinked, trying to process this information. "So now they last longer, talk, and can move things around?"

"Dude, let's get to the pond. You won't even believe it."

Ten minutes later they crested the ridge, allowing a clear view of the houseboat.

"Holy crap," Nico whispered.

"Yup."

Figments. Everywhere. Nico could see at least a dozen of them surrounding the water.

"Ty," Nico breathed, his pulse ratcheting up a notch. "What'd you guys do?"

"Don't look at me!" Tyler grumbled. "I made one BB-8, and the stupid droid tried to shock me before rolling into the bushes." He swept a hand at the circus by the lake. "This right here is the Emma Fairington show, and it runs nonstop."

Something uncomfortably tall with skinny arms and legs bounded toward them in bendy, knee-jarring lunges. Nico squinted, then straightened in astonishment. "Is that . . . is that an Elf on the Shelf?"

"Oh, his name is Herbie. When he gets up here, he'll tell you all about himself."

"Pass." Nico descended in the other direction, avoiding the prancing North Pole spy, who spun to face them as they climbed down. "I don't like how they watch us now."

Tyler snorted at his side. "That dead-eyed creep factory

117

isn't the worst. There was a giant chicken nugget earlier that just rolled around in circles, and a dozen ballerina pixies flying in attack formation. It's been quite an afternoon."

They reached the grassy field. Nico dodged a troop of Minions carrying saxophones but reared back as the pond's surface spluttered beside him. Out came a frogman in a tuxedo.

"*You're my bud! I'm your pal! We're a team and play we shall!*" The figment kicked up its feet and began to dance as Nico retreated, shaking his head and mumbling, "Nope nope nope." The frogman closed the distance, shouting, "*Friends are for caring and sharing!*"

Nico whispered harshly to Tyler. "Let's get out of here!"

"No argument here." They broke into a sprint for the stepping-stones.

"*Friends are fun, and you're a fun friend!*" the frogman shouted, swinging its arms as if marching in a parade.

Seconds later Emma emerged from the water in her bathing suit, lips blue, her body shaking from cold. "Nico! Did you see? The figments talk now! They last longer, too!"

"Inside the houseboat," Nico demanded. "We have *got* to talk, Emma."

Emma made a disappointed face but nodded. "Just keep an eye out for a centaur. I always wanted to ride one, but I hear they can be prickly."

"You've got to *slooooow* down." Tyler paced up and down the showroom aisle, waving his hands as he spoke. "It's like a riot out there, and some of these figments are getting weird around people."

"They're harmless." Emma sat on a full-size wooden carousel horse she'd found under a tarp. She seemed unconcerned by Tyler's histrionics. "We agreed to test the Darkdeep, right? Well, how else are we supposed to do it? I'm happy taking turns, but you go in once and then quit."

"A pair of Minecraft skeletons tied my shoelaces together," Tyler shot back. "I'm not leaving this room again until every last one of those things is gone."

"They're so much stronger now." Nico leaned against a bulky cabinet. Beside him, the green thing was slowly rotating in its jar. Nico wasn't sure, but it seemed even more solid. The center mass now had lumpy appendages. And was it shinier than before?

Emma's voice pulled him back. "The figments get stronger every dive we make. That's why we should keep going. Who knows what they'll be able to do soon?"

Tyler stared at her. "That's exactly why we should *stop*."

Nico found himself nodding. Something about what Emma had said made his skin crawl. But before he could explore that feeling, the curtain parted and Opal walked in.

Tyler stopped dead. "Okay, how'd you get here? Do you have another boat?"

"I told you, I have my ways." Opal winked, then crossed

119

the room to give Emma's fake horse a pat on the nose, but her smirk only lasted a moment. "Have you seen the centaur outside? It bowed to me and declared me its champion." Her voice dropped. "I touched its head, you guys. It felt . . . soft. So real."

"Ah, *dangit*. That was supposed to be *my* champion." Emma dropped to the floor. "Let's go say hi."

"Wait!" Nico pushed off the cabinet. "We need to decide how to manage these figments. They last longer, which means there could be dozens out there at a time if we're not careful."

"Making this island a magical paradise," Emma supplied, her blue eyes glowing with excitement. "I'm still waiting to hear the problem."

"You're *being* the problem!" Nico exploded. "You're seriously overdoing it, Emma."

Emma's face reddened. She crossed her arms but didn't respond.

"I have other news, too," Opal said quietly. Her gaze flicked to Nico. "It's not good."

Nico's hands found his pockets. "Well?"

Opal cleared her throat. "Logan has started asking questions."

Nico felt his blood pressure rise, but Opal continued before he could speak. "I ran into him at the radish pageant meeting, and he started badgering me about where I've been lately. That's hard to play off, guys. Suddenly I'm gone every afternoon, and anyone paying attention can see me biking into the hills."

"Logan's entering the pageant?" Tyler asked in disbelief. "I'm hearing that right?"

"What's his talent?" Emma asked. "I saw him logroll once, and he was pretty—"

"I don't care what Logan thinks." Nico tugged on his windbreaker with both hands, aiming a pointed look at Opal. "If you're gonna hang out with him all the time, tell him we're fishing in the state park. To the west."

"I'm not *hanging out* with him." Opal squeezed her long black braid. "It's a small town, Nico. You might be able to sneak away all the time with no one asking questions, but it's harder for some of us."

Nico's chest caved.

Opal paled. "Nico, I didn't mean—"

"It's fine." He waved it away. "You're right, I know." Nico took a deep breath. "Maybe we should shut everything down for a bit. Take a day off. I bet Ty and Emma have been skating on thin ice with these trips, too." He looked at his friends.

Tyler sighed. "My mom *is* getting annoyed. Coming up with excuses every day is tough."

Emma's shoulders drooped. "It's been a little tricky not being around to help out at the store. Not that I care!"

"It's settled, then." Nico felt relief steal over him. "We'll take a break and come up with a better plan for the Darkdeep." Opal frowned, and Emma looked ready to protest, so Nico added quickly, "After which, we'll keep testing it like we agreed."

Emma nodded, mollified. She laced her fingers together and batted her eyelashes. "Can I go one last time today? *Pleeeeease?*"

Tyler huffed loudly, but Nico chuckled. "Whatever. Make a troop of spider monkeys. But then we head back."

Emma squealed in delight, racing for the stairs. "Thanks, guys! I love being a Steward of the Midnight Pool!" She disappeared behind the wall.

Nico spun on Opal. "And now *you're* going to tell us how you keep getting out here all alone." He crossed his arms. "No more secrets, Opal. We're a team, right? So fess up. Do you have a jet pack or something?"

Opal laughed. "Nothing like that. But I do have something to show you."

Nico had thought the island couldn't surprise him anymore. He was wrong. The boys were peppering Opal with questions about her mystery tunnel when the houseboat lurched.

"What was that?" Opal asked.

Before anyone could answer, a shout carried in from outside.

"HELP!"

Nico felt his blood freeze.

It was Emma.

16

OPAL

They ran to the front porch.

Pulled up short, and stared.

A towering humanoid stood beside the pond, between Emma and the stepping-stones. The figment had shiny gray skin and impossibly long fingers. Opal spotted two extra eyes on the back of its head.

"Holy crap," Tyler breathed. "She made a Visitor."

"It's her favorite invasion show." Nico gripped his hair with both hands. "It only lasted twelve episodes, but Emma's seen them a million times."

Emma was trying to get around the figment, but it was between her and the stepping-stones, mirroring her every movement. "It won't let me back to the boat!" Even across the pond, Opal could hear the frustration in Emma's voice. "I don't understand. It's supposed to *help* me, like on the show!"

"Can we reach her?" Opal asked.

"Only one way to find out." Gritting his teeth, Tyler started out across the stones. Opal admired how he always pushed aside his fears when it came to Emma. They had an unshakable bond, just like with Nico. *Would any of them come for* me?

"Hey!" Nico called to the Visitor, waving his arms. "Over here!"

The Visitor didn't react. It continued to copy Emma, thwarting her moves.

"Get out of my way!" Emma yelled, stomping her foot. The Visitor stomped, too.

"Move it, spaceman!" Tyler shouted.

"Just go away!" Nico added. The Visitor ignored them both.

Opal caught up to the boys at the edge of the water. "We *said*, let her go!"

No.

Opal felt the word rather than heard it—a pulse that reverberated through her. What was going on? She got a very bad feeling in the pit of her stomach.

"Okay." Opal rubbed damp palms on her jeans. "Time to get the heck out of here."

"How?" Nico whispered. "Through your tunnel?"

Opal shook her head. "It's on the other side of the pond. But Visitors can't swim. It's one of their only weaknesses."

Nico shot her a skeptical look. "You're *sure* that thing can't swim?"

"I watched all twelve episodes, too!"

Tyler began edging around the Visitor. The eyes in the back of its head tracked him, but it made no move. The figment was focused on Emma, who'd given up trying to pass it.

Opal caught her eye and mouthed the word *beach*. Emma bit her lip. Nodded.

"We have to get its attention," Nico whispered.

"It doesn't care about us." Tyler waved at the monster. "See? Nothing."

"We should rush Emma," Opal said. "If we attack her, then it might notice us. She could sneak away."

No one spoke for a moment.

"Right," Nico said. "Let's try it. What's the worst that could happen?"

Tyler winced, squeezed his nose. "Nico, man. Please. Don't say stuff like that."

"It could dismember us." Opal giggled nervously. "A Visitor did that in episode four."

Tyler sagged. "You two are the worst."

"It's only a figment," Nico said, though it seemed as much to himself as to her and Tyler. "It can't actually do anything. Even the newer ones just kick sand and talk too much."

So far, Opal thought.

"You okay, Emma?" Tyler called out.

"Yeah." But she'd dropped into a fight-or-flight crouch. The Visitor mimicked her. Opal could tell Emma was nervous.

"Enough." Opal put her hands on her hips. "Let's do it.

125

Forget circling. We fire right down the middle, then scatter. Everyone meets back at the rowboat. Got it?"

"On three." Nico took a deep breath. "One. Two. *Three!*"

They shot past the Visitor, sprinting for their friend. Tyler yelled, "I'm coming, Emma!" Nico opted for a roar, while Opal shrieked like a banshee, waving her hands over her head. They met at Emma and yanked on her arms.

NO.

The Visitor surged forward. "Emma, run!" Tyler screamed. She sprinted for the woods. Nico and Tyler bolted along the edge of the pond.

Opal held her ground, waving at the Visitor while the others sped off. It frowned down at her, wriggling its spindly fingers. Then it stiffened. The figment's back-of-the-head eyes had spotted Emma running away.

NO!

"Move, Opal!" Nico shouted. He and Tyler banked like birds and tore into the trees. Opal shot after them, bringing up the rear. The Visitor chased them all with long, fluid steps.

Opal sprinted through the woods, lungs burning, feet flying over the uneven ground. She topped the ridge and glanced back. The Visitor was crashing through the forest canopy.

NO NO NO.

Branches snapped, showering Opal in an explosion of leaves and broken pine needles. She heard a tree trunk crash to the ground right behind her. *I'm not gonna make it.* But the woods thinned and she spotted Emma staggering across the beach. "Get into the cove!" Opal shouted.

Emma plunged into the ocean. Opal dove in after her, the cold stealing her breath.

The Visitor stopped at the waterline, watching the girls swim out of reach. Then it turned. Nico and Tyler were frantically shoving the rowboat into the surf, its keel grinding across rocks and sand. The Visitor stomped toward them.

Opal bobbed next to Emma. The boys were muscling the boat with every ounce of strength they possessed. Finally, it caught the tide and slid out to sea.

The Visitor stopped moving. It turned and watched Emma with liquid oval eyes.

Sorry.

Again, Opal didn't *hear* the word.

"Sorry for what?" Emma whispered. She'd felt it, too.

As they watched, the Visitor shimmered and vanished. Nico and Tyler paddled over and helped them slither aboard. The group collapsed in a tangled heap at the bottom of the boat, unable to muster the energy to even complain.

"Whoa," Emma said finally. "That was the best one yet."

"The *best* one?" Nico covered his eyes. "Are you kidding me?"

"It was so *real*," Emma breathed. "It didn't seem like a figment at all."

"I'm just glad it's gone." Tyler shuddered. "I'm glad they're all gone."

Opal ran a hand over her face. Setting an oar, she glanced back at the beach.

And froze.

"Guys. *Look.*"

They all turned.

"What. On. Earth," Tyler whispered.

Figments were emerging from the woods.

A centaur. A frog with a top hat. The Elf on a Shelf.

They stood in a line across the sand. Unspeaking. Unblinking.

Watching.

A sliver of fear entered Emma's voice.

"Oh," she said. "So they're not *all* gone."

PART THREE
THE TUNNEL

17

NICO

Nico was ready to go home.

Ready to forget about the bizarre new figments roaming the island, staring at them with creepy eyes. But Opal insisted they go back to the houseboat immediately. She wanted to talk, *now*, while they were still together.

So she showed them the tunnel.

It was right where she'd said it would be—in the back of the cave, where the rowboat had been hidden. The passage was a dingy, dusty, creepy mess, but it was there. Despite everything, Nico smiled in the darkness. Now they wouldn't have to row across Still Cove every time. No more staring down into the black water, imagining what might be looking up at you.

He wished Opal had told them sooner. He almost said something, but her face stopped him. It was like she *expected* him to bring it up. He'd surprise her by playing it cool. Truth was, Nico understood why she'd waited. He'd have done the same in her shoes.

The tunnel was rough but clearly manmade. They used phone lights to see, four harsh white circles burrowing down into the black. Reaching a straight passage at the bottom of the switchbacks, Nico realized they were *under* the cove. *Opal came through here alone? Wow.*

After a hundred paces they entered an open chamber. Opal continued without stopping, but Nico's feet slowed. "Wait," he called out. The others halted. Opal walked a few steps back into the chamber. "Something wrong?"

"What is this room?" Nico swung his light, illuminating a smooth, circular stone wall. The masonry was more refined here than in the narrow passage.

"I've never really looked," Opal admitted. "I don't like being down here alone."

Nico's light dipped, and he noticed a carving chiseled into the stone floor. It looked like a hand holding a torch. He tried to imagine who'd sat down here in the dark, chipping the design into the unyielding granite. Nico shivered. "Never mind. Let's keep moving."

The tunnel continued for another narrow stretch, then began climbing as sharply as it had dropped. Nico was ready for sunlight. Even the oppressive, foggy island was better than this. He was happy the tunnel existed but knew he'd never enjoy using it.

They emerged into a gully Nico hadn't explored. He gave Opal props—her showing up without explanation had been driving him crazy, and walking that path alone took guts.

Thankfully, the area around the pond was figment free. Gasping sighs of relief, they hustled into the houseboat as the sun began to set. Nico fervently hoped all the creatures were gone. He didn't want to feel their stares again.

Inside the showroom, Opal wheeled on the group, arms latched across her chest. "Okay, we *seriously* need to talk."

Emma scuffed a sneaker on the fraying carpet. Though he couldn't believe it, Nico caught her eyeing the hidden entrance to the Darkdeep. "Sorry about the last one," she mumbled to the floor. "I got greedy. I won't think of anything that scary again."

"It's not really about scary," Opal said. "The Visitor was *aggressive*. It was blocking you, Emma. And I . . . I think it spoke inside my head."

Opal's gaze darted from face to face, stopping on Nico. He nodded. He'd felt it, too.

Emma's head snapped up. "But isn't that a good thing? The figments are getting more real. More interactive. More amazing! Guys, we might be able to do things with them soon. Or learn where they come from. Or . . . or . . . *anything*."

"We know where they come from." Tyler glared at his friend. He seemed near the end of his rope. "They come from a spinning, mind-reading, houseboat-basement whirlpool! Which isn't possible. *None of this is possible*. Can't you see things are out of control?"

He was breathing hard by the time he finished. Silence filled the room. Emma couldn't meet Tyler's eye. Glancing away, Nico noticed the pedestal jar. The thing inside had changed yet again, and the water was emitting a dim light of its own.

Nico pointed, but Opal wasn't interested in distractions.

"We don't know what we're dealing with," she said. "At first it was just a neat trick. The Darkdeep read our minds and made funny images of our thoughts. But it's obviously stronger than that. The new figments are *doing* stuff. That Visitor knocked over a tree. What if one of us had been underneath it?"

"I said I was sorry," Emma muttered.

Tyler squeezed her shoulder. "Stop it. We know. Nobody's blaming you." He shot a hard look at Opal.

"Definitely not blaming," Opal agreed, color rising in her cheeks. "We all were doing it, Emma. I'm just saying we need to learn more before we go any further."

"What do you mean?" Nico asked. Opal's suggestion had him curious.

Opal inhaled and exhaled deeply. "I think we should do some research."

Nico laughed. "Sure. I'll google 'houseboat vortexes' while you buy a copy of *How to Deal with Prancing Figments*."

Opal gave him a level look. "Have you considered where we're standing?"

Nico's eyes traveled the showroom. "Of course."

"And what were we doing before we found the pool?"

"Making an inventory," Nico said defensively. *What's she getting at?*

Opal tilted her head to the side. "How much of that task did we accomplish?"

Nico held his tongue, refusing the bait. Tyler looked sheepish. "Not much," he said.

Opal smiled triumphantly. "*So . . .* did it occur to anyone else that a collection like this might have information regarding the supernatural spin-cycle downstairs?"

Nico's toes curled in his shoes. Nodding in surrender, he surveyed the room with fresh eyes. "We should check everything—boxes, crates, chests, whatever. List all the books we find, then scan their headings and indexes. Look for anything about the Darkdeep."

Emma brightened. "*Backstory*. Yes. A place like this must have an incredible history."

"Look for stuff about this island, too," Opal added. "Also whoever built the houseboat, or assembled the collection. There's no way it doesn't all fit together."

"Don't forget the tunnel," Tyler chimed in. "Shoot, anything about Still Cove at all."

Energized, they split into pairs, Opal and Nico attacking a heap of books inside a huge orange trunk while Emma and Tyler rifled through dusty cabinets. Soon they were calling out titles to one another, making group decisions on how to sort them.

"*Weapons of the Nineteenth Century?*" Emma announced.

Opal pursed her lips. "Hmmm. Stick it in the 'Unlikely' pile."

Tyler blew a cloud of dust from the cover of another volume. "*A Topographical Survey of the Washington Coastline.* Might be something about Still Cove in here."

Nico nodded. "That's a definite 'Maybe.'"

Tyler was placing the book on a stack when Opal squealed. "Guys! Listen!" She held up a moth-eaten tome that looked older than all the others. "*Natural Forces and Phantasms: Science of the Mind Realms.*"

"That one's smoking hot!" Nico called out. "Make a new pile."

And so it went for a half hour, until most of the books were sorted. Yawning, Nico scratched the back of his head. They'd found some decent leads. In addition to Opal's find, there were three history books about Timbers, a collection of Skagit Sound legends, a set of houseboat schematics, and a leather notebook with *Torchbearer's Log* branded on its cover.

But nothing specifically about the pool. Nico couldn't help feeling disappointed. Then he chastised himself. *What'd you expect, a book called* Darkdeep for Dummies? "We'll start with these and see if they spark anything," he said, trying to sound upbeat.

Emma smiled over-big, wheedling like a saleswoman. "And the Darkdeep tests? Steady as we go?"

"That's not a good idea," Nico said. "Opal's right about us being in over our heads. Let's figure out what the Darkdeep is before making any more figments. Deal?"

Emma's expression soured. "Then let's get reading."

"Tonight?" Tyler glanced at his watch. "It's dark already, and we've got school." He went to the lone window. "I don't see any figments, but a few could still be around. Are we starting this now or heading home?"

Nico checked his phone. No messages, but no service either. "I'm willing to stick around for a bit."

"My mom has book club tonight," Opal said. "That buys me two more hours."

Emma shrugged. "My parents went to a movie. I've got until ten at least." Tyler groaned theatrically, but settled down on the floor. "Research party!" Emma crowed, and the others laughed.

"I'm gonna read *Forces and Phantasms*." Opal was already digging into the pile. "I want to know why some figments last hours while others vanish sooner."

"I have a theory about that," Nico offered quietly.

Opal paused. "Oh?"

Nico swiped at his nose, suddenly self-conscious. "It's nothing. I just think maybe the big ones might take more . . . *energy*, you know? Like, they're stronger, but can't last as long because of it. So the smaller figments hold together more easily, but the large ones burn out."

Opal chewed the inside of her cheek. "But some little ones have disappeared fast, too."

Nico looked away. "It was only an idea. I'm probably wrong."

"No, no." Opal nodded encouragingly. "I think you're onto something. It's obvious the first figments were weaker than more recent ones. Maybe size plays into it, too." Wrinkling her nose, she slapped the book in her lap. "I hope this tells me. I want to know *everything* about the Darkdeep."

"Me too," Nico said. They smiled at each other. To Nico, it felt like the first relaxed moment they'd shared since grade school. It was nice being back on good terms with Opal. He hadn't realized how much he'd missed being friends with her.

A second later, the curtain parted.

Logan Nantes walked into the showroom.

18

OPAL

This is even creepier than your house, Holland."

Logan sauntered down the aisle like he owned the place. But Opal saw his eyes widen as he took it all in.

Emma was the first to find her voice. "What are you doing here?" she sputtered.

Tyler and Nico looked like they'd been struck by lightning. Their eyes darted to Opal, and her stomach sank. They were going to blame her for this.

"This isn't *your* boat, is it?" Logan picked up a turquoise glass elephant and bounced it in one hand. Opal hoped he'd cut himself. "I didn't see a NO TRESPASSING sign."

Opal took a deep breath. "How'd you get here, Logan?"

"Followed you." He met her eye briefly before looking away. Did she see hurt there, behind the anger? "It's obvious you've been hiding something, ever since Holland lost his crappy drone."

"*You*—" Tyler began, but Logan spoke over him.

"I knew you were out here somewhere." He glanced at Opal again, and whatever she'd seen a moment ago was gone, replaced by a mean smirk. "I didn't think you'd actually climb down into Still Cove, though. *Wow*. I almost gave up on the cliffs, but then I saw footprints in the mud and found that ridiculous suicide path. When I got to the bottom I heard your voices, found the cave, the tunnel, and *boom*." He dropped the elephant on the carpet. "Here I am."

"Get out." Nico took a step toward Logan and pointed at the curtain. "*Now*."

"No. I don't want to, and you can't make me." Logan lifted a book from the 'Maybe' stack and flipped the pages roughly. "What *is* this place, anyway? What's with all the junk?"

"Give me that, Logan." Opal stepped in front of him and held out her hand.

He snorted and walked past her.

Nico hurried to Opal's side. "Did you tell him?" he hissed.

She felt Tyler and Emma watching. "No!" Opal folded her arms. "*Logan*. Put the book down."

"Dear Diary," Logan whined, pretending to read. "My name is Nico. All my friends are dorks. Also, I'm in *loooove* with Opal Walsh. How can I get her to like me? Maybe if I take her to a secret trash barge, she'll—"

"*Shut up*," Opal spat. Any sympathy she'd felt for Logan vaporized.

Logan closed the book. Opal nearly sighed in relief as he set it back where he'd found it. But his words had been a slap to all of them. The tension in the room was choking.

Logan's eyebrows rose as he peered past Opal. She followed his gaze. In its jar atop the pedestal, the strange green thing was floating upright. Two dark spots had appeared. They looked like eyes.

"Gross." Logan strode over and knocked on the glass. "You guys steal this from a bio lab?"

Opal stormed forward and grabbed his arm. "Don't touch anything."

Logan gave her an icy glare. "Hands off, Walsh."

He's using my last name now, too.

Opal tightened her grip. "You need to go. You don't belong here."

Logan flinched. "And you do?"

Emma and Tyler hurried around the pedestal, blocking Logan's view of the back wall. But Tyler kept glancing over his shoulder. "Just stay . . . stay where you are!"

"Oh, wow." Logan pulled free of Opal's grasp. "Are you *hiding* something?" He pushed past Tyler and Emma. "Whaddya got? A hidden vault full of gold doubloons?"

He rapped a fist against the wall. The panel popped open, revealing the staircase.

Logan stepped back in surprise. "Oh, crap. I was kidding."

"It's just the hold." Emma shrugged, feigning nonchalance.

"Go ahead if you want, but I'm not coming with you." She made a scurrying motion with her fingers. "Spiders."

The ploy almost worked. Logan squinted into the darkness as if having second thoughts. Then he clicked his tongue. "Yeah, right." His shoes rang on the stairs like warning chimes as he headed for the basement.

"Logan!" Opal raced after him, the others trailing behind. "Hey, *seriously*. It's not safe down there!"

She took the steps two at a time, tripping on the last one and staggering into Logan, who stood at the Darkdeep's edge. "What is this?" he whispered, ignoring the collision.

"Nothing," Tyler said reflexively.

"A well," Emma answered at the same time.

"Something that can hurt you." Nico was the last to reach the bottom. "Trust me, Logan. That water is dangerous."

"Right. Trust *you*." Logan began to circle the pool. "Why is it moving like that?"

Opal stood statue-still, not daring to answer. *What if he touches the water?*

"This is your fault," Nico hissed at her.

"I didn't invite him!" Opal's hands were shaking. Logan stared into the Darkdeep with a predatory gleam.

Nico's eyes blazed. "He followed *you*."

Emma looked away. Emotions warred on Tyler's face, but he didn't say anything.

Opal couldn't breathe with the unfairness of it all. They

were holding her responsible for Logan's actions. Why was *she* guilty for what he did? *No.* She answered for herself and no one else. "I am *tired* of you doing this to me," Opal spat through gritted teeth.

Nico flinched. His mouth opened.

"Doing what?" Logan had come full circle. "Are your friends being mean, Opal?" He'd said her first name this time, but that meant nothing. Not with that taunt in his voice. Not after he'd stalked her across Timbers and ruined everything.

"Get out of here, Logan," Opal said.

"Not a chance." He pointed at the churning water. "I want to know what this pool is, and why you're being so weird about it." His tone became mocking. "Will it turn me into Spider-Man or something?"

Nico raised a palm. "I promise you, that well is toxic. You need to stay away from it."

"I *almost* believe you, Holland." Logan smiled wryly. "The problem is you're a wimp."

He knelt and reached toward the water.

"No!" Opal rushed at Logan. She *had* to stop him.

Nico got there first. He grabbed Logan's arm and yanked it back.

"Get off me!" Logan tried to shove him away, but Nico held on, and the motion knocked them both off balance.

"Look out!" Opal cried.

Locked arm in arm, the two boys tipped, toppled, fell.

Logan touched the surface first. For a moment, the dark water stilled.

Then it swallowed them whole.

19

NICO

Nico felt the cold of the Darkdeep envelop him.

His body seized as he was dragged down into the bottomless black. A pulse of energy ran over him, *through* him. He wanted to scream, but suffocating liquid pressed in from all sides. He was drenched. He was frozen. He was unmade.

Then it all vanished. He floated in a void. Days. Seconds. An instant.

Like the times before, but also . . . different.

He felt another presence struggling with him. Lashing. Twisting. Panicking.

Logan?

The sensation flickered. Currents of pure emptiness scattered Nico's thoughts.

Beneath them, Nico sensed a deeper awareness.

Something murky. Alien. Impossibly old.

The Darkdeep wrapped around him like a funeral

shroud, then tightened, enfolding Nico in a net of midnight black.

His mind blanked, and he felt nothing more.

Nico awoke gasping and spitting by the pond. He rolled onto his back.

"Oh, man," he rasped. "Oh, jeez."

He'd been through the vortex a dozen times, but this trip had been a nightmare. His head suddenly weighed fifty pounds. His fingers were blue, his body chilled to ice-cube status.

Nico had never felt so powerless inside the Darkdeep.

He'd never felt someone else.

He rocketed up. Spotted Logan a stone's throw away—he'd crawled halfway out of the pond and wasn't moving. Nico scrambled over to him, shouting his name.

Logan didn't respond.

Nico reached for him but stopped short.

Should I touch him? What if he has internal injuries?

"Hold on, man." Nico twisted around. A full moon was rising beyond the fog, casting an eerie half-light over the island. He spotted Opal leaping across the stones, Tyler and Emma hot on her heels.

"Over here!" Nico waved, then turned back to Logan, who groaned and licked his lips. Nico's heart started beating again. "Just relax, dude. We'll get you fixed up. Don't . . . don't freak out or anything."

Logan puked into the grass. "Wha . . . what happened?"

"We fell into the Dar"—Nico winced—"the pool under the boat. Came up in the pond. You'll be fine in a minute." But Nico wasn't sure. No one had gone through the Darkdeep with another person before.

Opal and the others were racing toward them. Nico stood. Cracked his neck. A moment later the ground shuddered beneath his feet.

Nico froze. "What was . . ."

The island went silent.

The hairs on his neck stood.

Logan hocked onto the grass. "Oh man, I feel like a used Kleenex." He rose to his knees, then shot Nico a wild-eyed look. "What's going on? What was that . . . that *thing* in the water? What are you guys doing out here?"

"*Shhh.*" Nico waved for quiet. "Something isn't right."

"*Of course it's not right!*" Logan staggered to his feet. "I got sucked down some kind of undertow . . . into . . . into . . ." He aimed a finger at Nico. "Tell me *right now* what you and your weirdo friends are up to, or—"

The ground shook a second time.

"Be quiet, Logan!" Nico tried to look everywhere at once. "You don't understand what's happening. We should get back to the houseboat."

147

"Where the whirlpool is?" Logan stared at Nico in horror. "No way. I'm not going near that thing." His teeth chattered. "Did you . . . I swear I felt something. Like there was someone in the water with us."

A tree groaned. There was a sound like a bullwhip, then a broken sentinel pine crashed to the mud less than a dozen yards from where they stood.

"Oh no," Nico whispered.

"What was *that*?" Logan shouted, his voice cracking.

From the gloom emerged a giant, clanking monstrosity. It stood fifteen feet tall, wearing a dark robe with the hood thrown back. A smell like rotten eggs swept the field.

Moonlight pierced the mists, illuminating the figment's face. Beady black eyes flanked a veiny, bulbous nose. Two sharp tusks protruded from its mouth.

"No!" Logan stumbled backward in shock. "You can't be real! I stopped playing years ago, I promise!"

Nico's eyes shot to his companion. "What is that?"

"Volg," Logan practically whimpered. "It's the Ogre King."

The nightmare glared down with scorching eyes. "*Invaders*," it growled through dripping jaws, though its voice sounded mechanized. "Humans have no place in my empire!" Lightning bolts sizzled along the creature's sleeves as it unsheathed an enormous broadsword and raised it with an earthshaking roar. Fire erupted from the blade.

Nico gasped, his blood turning to ice. "Holy crap. That's no ogre!"

Thanks to the burning sword and electric robe, Nico could better see the creature's face. Its skin was made of liquid metal. The tusks were steel spikes. The letter *M* was stamped in the center of its forehead.

"That's Mordan," Nico whispered, his jaw dropping open. "Warden of the Ways."

Nico used to watch Japanese cartoons with his older brother as a kid. Mordan was a robot monk tasked with guarding the underworld on the planet Hexra. Mordan had scared Nico witless every time he saw him. After three episodes and a dozen nightmares, Nico never watched the show again.

Yet here the robot god was. Only . . . why did he also look like an ogre?

Logan was nearly hyperventilating at Nico's side. He'd backpedaled into the pond up to his ankles, but didn't seem to notice. "*Ogre Wars* is just a stupid video game. I quit when I was ten!" His hand shot out to grip Nico's arm. "Why am I seeing Volg? Why is he made of metal?"

"Volg? That's Mordan. You can tell by . . ."

Then it hit him.

Two people had gone into the Darkdeep. One horrible figment came out.

"You have sullied Hexra's burial ground!" Volg/Mordan

thundered. "The war continues! You shall be *DESTROYED*."
The creature reversed the flaming sword and drove it into the
ground.

That was enough for both of them.

"Run!" Nico shouted, matching action to words. Logan
was a step behind him.

Air swooshed over Nico's head. He heard a bone-jarring
thwack, followed by the hum of quivering metal.

"It's trying to kill us!" Logan shouted, nearly face-planting
in panic. Nico grabbed his elbow to steady him and risked a
backward glance. The sword was stuck in the belly of an oak
tree. Huge robot arms were straining to free it.

It is *trying to kill us. A figment! What is happening?*

They ran smack into Opal, Tyler, and Emma at the edge
of the pond.

"Back back back!" Nico shouted. "This one's homicidal!"

The others spun on a dime, but Logan stopped dead. He
stared at Nico, wide-eyed and panting like a spooked race-
horse. "This one? What do you mean, *this one*?"

Nico seized Logan by the shoulder. "Now is not the time!
We'll wait this thing out on the houseboat."

Logan lurched free. "You're crazy," he whispered. "All of
you!" Before anyone could stop him, Logan shot past the
stepping-stones, tearing around the back side of the pond
toward the gully that hid the tunnel. Away from the bellow-
ing ogre god with a razor-sharp sword.

"Inside, right now!" Nico shouted.

"What about Logan?" Opal said.

"What about *us*?" Tyler shot back. Emma was already on the second stone, bounding for the boat. The others followed like a ragged flock of birds.

Nico heard something crunch behind him, then a furious roar. He didn't stop. Didn't look back. Didn't take a single breath until his sneakers hit the porch. There he whirled, terrified he'd see a fiery broadsword slicing toward his throat.

But the figment was mired near the shoreline. It had one foot on dry land, the other in the pond. The first stepping-stone had cracked under its weight and its left leg was now buried in the mud. The creature's robe sparked and hissed. Its fiery sword went out. Volg/Mordan bellowed in fury. It took another step, sinking to the waist.

"Too heavy!" Tyler nearly sobbed in relief. "Maybe it can't reach us."

The robot ogre dragged itself out and stood dripping in the darkness, staring at the houseboat. A growl carried across the water. The creature began to circle the pond.

"There's no other way to the houseboat," Nico said, trying to slow his rampaging pulse. "I . . . I think we're safe. Unless Volg/Mordan can fly." He laughed nervously.

"Volg? Mordan?" Opal wiped sweat from her forehead. "What are you talking about?"

Nico felt the adrenaline leaking out of him. "I'll explain

inside. We're stuck here until that monster disappears anyway."

It took *two hours* for the figment to vanish—even though it was huge, could speak, and was trashing the world around it. Nico explained his theory about the double monster—that it sprang from his and Logan's imaginations combined. As the robot ogre circled, slamming its sword into the ground, the group dug into the books they'd gathered, looking for anything about the Darkdeep.

Nico was sitting by the window when the monster finally disappeared. He felt the ghostly tickle of a sword swinging for his neck. Broke out into a sweat.

The creature outside might be gone, but the warning was inescapable.

A figment had tried to kill him.

20

OPAL

> # ATTACK OF THE KILLER RADISHES—THIS SATURDAY!!!

The banner hung over the entrance to the Timbers Public Library across the street.

"What on earth does *that* mean?" Opal said. She wondered if she'd forgotten something. Had they conjured up walking vegetables at some point? Was she losing her mind?

"It's a horror movie." Emma gave an enthusiastic thumbs-up. "They're showing it the night of the festival, after the pageant."

"Killer radishes?" Nico squinted at the banner. "I thought it was tomatoes."

"That's actually the movie," Emma said. "But I'm going

to have a live mic, and every time anyone in the movie says 'tomatoes,' I'm supposed to shout 'RADISHES' over it."

"Wow." Tyler shook his head.

Emma nodded sagely. "It's lucky I know the lines so well."

They were sitting on the school steps. On every lamppost, smiling radish signs beamed at the residents of Timbers. But many of the adults seemed worried, like they were convinced the fate of Timbers was riding on the success of the festival. Almost everyone was involved in some way, including the kids. Most weren't as laid-back about it as Emma.

"We should meet again," Opal said. "That robot-ogre gave me nightmares. Things are bad, you guys."

"I know, but I can't right now." Nico rubbed his temple as if to ward off a headache. "My dad got home before I did last night and yelled at me for being late. Plus I have a costume fitting for the parade."

"Could be worse." Opal squeezed her eyes shut. "I have a private dance rehearsal. My mom wants to see my routine."

Nico snorted. "What about you, Ty? What have they roped you into?"

"The radish-eating contest." Tyler covered his face. "My mom's in charge of it."

Emma cringed. "That's disgusting. Everyone's gonna be sick."

Tyler chuckled grimly. "Somebody bring the barf bags, is all I'm saying."

Opal laughed. It was all so ridiculous, wasting time on this nonsense after what they'd seen yesterday. What they'd *made*.

"This festival is doomed," Emma said cheerfully. "So many bad ideas at once."

Opal undid the rubber band at the end of her braid and started fixing it again. "I mean, radishes are fine, I guess. They're a pretty color. I know Timbers ships a lot of them to restaurants in Seattle. But this was the *best* idea the town could come up with?"

"What *is* the best thing about Timbers?" Nico asked. Opal detected a current of bitterness in his voice.

"All of it," Opal answered, surprising herself. When Nico glanced at her, she searched for the right words. "The radish farmers, the mill, everything." Opal held out her arms, trying to encompass the whole town. Main Street and its old-fashioned streetlights. Overlook Row, with its beautiful painted houses facing the sea. The chalkboard sign outside the coffee shop listing the daily specials. The slumping pier, the green parks, the redbrick library. The mountains, the sky, the fields and woods.

If this isn't enough, what is?

"It's just a really nice place to live." Opal felt a sudden swell of pride in her hometown. And panic that it might be in danger. She looked at Nico, and wondered if he was thinking the same thing.

"So here's what we need to do." Opal scooted closer to the

others so no one else could overhear. "First, we should go back to the houseboat and keep searching those books. Find out what we're dealing with."

"No more Darkdeeping," Emma said sadly.

Opal nodded. "Not until we know more."

Nico folded his arms. "And second, we need to decide what to do about Logan."

"Right." Opal sighed. The concrete steps chilled her legs through her jeans. A crumpled leaf skittered across her sneaker. "I'll talk to him." She was the only one he might listen to.

Logan had run off in a total panic last night. Who had he told? What would he do next?

Opal had been half-relieved when he didn't show up at school that morning—he couldn't blab to his friends if he wasn't there. But he might be at home right now, talking to his parents. Or the police. The FBI. Anyone. What if a SWAT team was motoring toward Still Cove right now, to investigate what Logan said?

"Speak of the devil." Tyler clicked his tongue. "Here he comes."

"What?" Opal turned around. She'd assumed she'd have time to gather her thoughts and approach Logan friend-to-friend. *Or person-to-person.* But his mother's BMW convertible was pulling into the parking lot.

"Crap," Opal said. To no one. The others had slunk off in various directions.

Cowards.

"Hi, Mrs. Nantes!" Opal called, as Logan's mother climbed out and shut the door. Opal's cheery voice sounded false even to her own ears.

Logan stayed in the car, staring straight ahead.

"Hello, Opal. Logan's not feeling well, so I'm letting the pageant director know he'll miss rehearsal. We're headed to the doctor." Mrs. Nantes sounded worried.

As soon as Mrs. Nantes stepped inside the school, Opal hurried down and knocked on the car window. Logan ignored her at first, so she pounded harder. *I'm not going away.* With a grimace, he finally lowered it. "What?" he said in a flat voice.

"I want to make sure you're okay." She tried to catch his eye, but he kept staring straight ahead through the windshield. "Please don't say anything about the houseboat, or what happened. Not before we can explain."

"About what happened."

"Yeah."

"We both know *what happened,* Opal." He looked at her then, eyes cold and scary. *Haunted.* "You and Nico tried to drown me. Then I had a mental breakdown."

"No. Logan, listen. You guys fell. After—"

"Look, I get it, okay? You got me back for the drone." Logan put his head down against the dashboard. "With your sick, creepy pool. I hope you're both proud. Something's wrong with me now. I . . . I thought . . . the worst things inside me keep . . ." He shuddered. "Leave me *alone*."

Logan rolled the window up in Opal's face.

She stood there, stunned. The glass between them felt a mile thick. Feeling awkward and upset, Opal hurried back to the school.

Logan didn't know it, but he'd pinpointed what frightened *her* about the Darkdeep.

Did the pool know who you really were? Your darkest thoughts, deep down inside?

Can it see what's wrong with me?

21

NICO

It looked like weather for the underworld.

Still Cove was usually just that—windless and dank—but frigid gusts that afternoon had Nico jamming his hands into his pockets. The fog swirled and danced rather than hanging like a wet sock.

Emma shivered as she exited the tunnel. "It's like an old black-and-white detective movie out here. Very film noir."

Tyler shot her an anxious look. "Don't those usually end badly?"

"Almost always."

"Great."

Opal emerged last and the group started up the rocky incline.

"Let's not waste time." Tyler blew into a fist as he climbed. "This gone-every-day stuff is getting on my parents' last nerves. If they weren't busy repainting the pier for the radish madness, I'd have been busted already."

"We sold out of camping chairs at the store," Emma said. "Even though Mom stocked way more than usual. Air horns, too. This could be the most obnoxious parade in history."

"Wonderful," Nico muttered. "I'll be dressed like a radish when my eardrums rupture."

Opal sniffed. "At least you don't have to dance like one."

The tunnel exit wasn't far from the pond, but on the opposite side, near the northern tip of the island. They could usually see the houseboat from the ridgetop, but a heavy mist was rising off the water like steam from a coffee mug. Opal hugged herself for warmth. "Do you think the showroom has a fireplace?"

Nico shrugged, zipping his jacket all the way. "Maybe there's an HVAC system. I'll look for the thermostat next time I'm in the laundry room."

Opal blinked at him, then barked a laugh. "Right. Check beside the vending machines."

Nico grinned, pleased he'd made Opal smile. He felt terrible about blaming her for Logan showing up. He'd apologized while they waited for the robot ogre to disappear, but hadn't been totally sure she'd accepted it.

They were a team now. Turning on each other was no longer an option. He'd forgotten that in the heat of the moment, but Nico didn't think Opal would have done the same. He vowed to never make that mistake again.

"What's so funny?" Tyler asked.

Opal glanced at Nico, still giggling, then waved the question away. "We're just trying to figure out the houseboat's Wi-Fi password."

Tyler's brow furrowed. "Darkdeep1234. Duh."

He laughed, and the others joined in. The group cracked up for a few moments, outside in the windy gloom. *Whatever else, we've got each other*, Nico thought. A small thing, but a big one, too.

Then a howl cut through the fog, killing the vibe.

Nico tensed like a hunted animal. "What's that?"

"Dunno," Tyler whispered, eyes roving. "Wolf?"

Opal shook her head. "If a wolf pack was living on the island, we'd know. They'd have introduced themselves by now."

"I think it came from downwind." Nico pointed in the direction of the pond, which was where they wanted to go. A second bloodcurdling wail echoed over the ridge.

"Okay, new plan." Tyler began backing toward the tunnel. "We run away and don't die."

Nico was about to agree when two scarlet circles appeared in the mist, freezing his blood and pinning his sneakers to the ground. "Uh-oh," Opal whispered, extending a shaky finger.

"Eyes," Emma whimpered. "Those are very unfriendly looking *eyes*."

The orbs regarded them silently for a moment, then floated closer. A gust swept the ridge, parting the fog to reveal a four-legged creature shaped like a rhinoceros but covered in spiky red fur. Two wicked horns protruded from its head.

Nico swallowed. "That's a figment. Who called it up?" When no one spoke, he shot an exasperated glance at the others. "We're through pointing fingers, but we need to know what this thing can do. Fess up, whoever made it."

The creature stamped a massive foot. Steam poured from its nostrils.

Still no one answered. Nico was about to repeat his question when the beast growled, swaying its head from side to side. "That's not good," Tyler whispered. "I watch a lot of Animal Planet. I think it's abo—"

The creature charged, closing the gap in an instant. Nico dove sideways and it pounded past him, horns thrust forward like deadly spikes. It skidded into the gully.

Nico scrambled back up, frantically searching for his friends. Opal had disappeared. Tyler and Emma were sprinting toward the pond. The creature was awkwardly turning around. Its roar shook the island.

Nico took off after Tyler and Emma.

He caught them on the field by the water. Glanced back. The enraged rhino had picked its way downslope and was thundering in pursuit. Nico realized they'd never reach the entry stones before it caught up.

"Into the woods!" he shouted. The trio hooked into the forest and raced for cover. The figment stampeded after them, snapping branches and ripping bushes apart as it battered a path through the trees. "Keep going!" Nico yelled. "That thing's a tank—it'll get stuck!" But from the sounds of destruction behind them, the trees weren't slowing it much.

"Where's Opal?" Emma yelled.

"I don't know! She must've gotten away. It's only after us!"

Nico desperately hoped that was true, but there was no time to investigate. The noise was getting closer. As they ran into the heart of the woods, Nico lost all sense of where they were. He worried they might accidentally run off a cliff.

They reached a hidden meadow. Nico led Emma and Tyler across as fast as he could, but the creature crashed from the trees a moment later, tossing its head and growling. Too late, Nico realized his mistake—he'd chosen open ground. They were sitting ducks.

Suddenly, Opal appeared at the opposite end of the field, waving her hands wildly. "Over here! Hurry!" Nico, Tyler, and Emma sprinted toward her.

The red rhino roared after them, tearing up the grass.

Then Opal did a crazy thing. She sprinted left, flapping her arms and screaming.

Nico nearly tripped in surprise. He and Tyler stumbled over a slight rise and abruptly felt air beneath their feet. They tumbled headfirst into a creek. A moment later Emma landed on top of them with a painful thud.

"*Ugh*," Nico groaned.

"I'm dead," Tyler wheezed. "You deaded me."

"Sorry!" Emma whispered.

Sucking wind, Nico watched Opal sprint along the rise shielding the creek from view. He couldn't see the enraged rhino, but Nico heard it—the creature slammed on the brakes not ten feet from where they crouched. With a roar it turned and shot after Opal, who'd stopped running and was fumbling with something on the ground. Then she started jumping up and down.

The monster charged directly at her.

She stopped jumping and went statue-still.

"Opal, no." Nico murmured, but the scene was out of his control.

The monster closed. Opal stood firm.

Right when it looked certain she'd be impaled and trampled, the figment disappeared.

Nico shot to his feet. "How did she know?"

A howl rattled his eardrums. Nico flinched, even more confused. Opal was standing right where she had been, hands on her knees as she took deep breaths. She was mumbling something with her eyes closed.

Nico helped Tyler and Emma out of the creek. "Come on!"

They raced over to Opal. She straightened and held up her hands. "Stop!"

Nico stumbled to a halt, throwing his arms out to stop his friends' momentum.

Then he saw it, and everything made sense.

A narrow trench split the ground. Opal was on the other side of it. The rhino had fallen into the ravine and was *not* happy about it. It bucked furiously, unable to climb out.

Opal gave a shaky grin. "I didn't want you to fall in, too. That would defeat the purpose."

Tyler stared at Opal in awe. "How did . . . ?"

Opal kicked a thick wooden board at her feet. "This was lying across the gap. When I got separated from you guys, I ran this direction, and then spotted Nico in the field." She flapped an aimless hand. "It just kinda came together."

"I'll say." Emma seemed starstruck. "You're like Lara Croft."

Opal snorted unsteadily. "I just about wet my pants."

Nico glanced down at the snarling figment. "Whose *is* this one, anyway? Did someone go through the Darkdeep after Logan and me? Or right before?"

The others shook their heads. Nico felt a moment's suspicion, but crushed it. They were done turning on each other. He trusted everyone in the group. Especially Opal, who'd just risked her life for them.

But then . . . where did the figment come from?

An answer came to him like a spear through the gut. "Logan."

"Impossible," Opal replied immediately. "I talked to him. He wouldn't come back. He's totally freaked out."

Nico scowled in disgust. "Who else, Opal? He's the only other person who knows about the Darkdeep, and he was AWOL all morning while we were at school."

Opal opened her mouth, then closed it. A look of concern crossed her face.

Emma spoke in a small voice. "What if it came on its own?"

Nico frowned. "That's impossible. Figments appear after someone goes in the whirlpool. That's how it works."

"Do we *know* that?" Emma regarded him with serious eyes. "We're guessing, about this whole thing."

"We need answers." Tyler pounded a fist into his palm. "For real this time. No more games, no playing around. Someone built the houseboat, which means they knew about the pool. They *had* to have left a record behind."

Opal nodded from across the gap. "I'm worried we started something we can't stop."

A popping sound made Nico jump. The figment had vanished. Tyler sighed in relief, but then froze mid-exhale, squinting into the ravine. "Guys? There's something else down there."

Nico leaned over the edge. "Ty's right. I think maybe it's a . . . jacket?"

"More than that." Emma's voice caught. "I see a person. Or what's left of one."

Opal looked down, then slid the board over the ravine and quickly walked across, releasing a pent-up breath when she reached them. Nico tapped his chin a moment, then pulled the board farther back until its far end dropped into the hole. Before anyone could protest, Nico angled the plank against the side of the ravine and scrambled down it like a ramp.

"Nico, *come on*," Tyler whined. "Haven't we had enough fun for today?"

Nico ignored him, heart pounding. "It's a skeleton," he finally managed.

The bones were still in proper arrangement, held together by a zipped-up canvas uniform and heavy men's winter jacket. It was a miracle the figment hadn't trampled them. A worn baseball cap sat beside the skeleton. Nico recognized its logo immediately, and his stomach sank. "This guy worked for Nantes Timber Company."

"Can you tell who it is?" Opal asked. "Like, is there a wallet or something?"

She wants me to touch it. But Nico knew he didn't have a choice. He reached into the jacket pockets. Nothing. So he swallowed and pulled on the uniform's zipper. It slid a few inches and got stuck. Nico stepped back, hastily wiping his hands on his jeans. "I didn't find anything."

"That's okay." Opal strangled her braid with both hands. "Nico, just come out of there. We shouldn't disturb the dead." Emma and Tyler nodded solemnly.

Nico removed his phone and took a couple of pics, just in case. He did *not* want to come down there again. He was about to climb back up the board—and shake out a serious case of the heebie-jeebies—when something around the skeleton's neck caught his eye.

Almost against his will, Nico knelt. The skeleton wore an ornament on a cord. It rested against a collarbone slashed by a puckered brown line, as if the bone had been broken once but never properly set. He took one last photo.

Something stirred the leaves at his feet and Nico lost his nerve. He leaped onto the board and darted up out of the ravine like something was chasing him. The others patted his back until the shivers subsided.

"What'd you see?" Emma asked.

"Necklace." Nico's mouth was dry. "I left it alone."

"Like the ones in those houseboat pictures?" Opal asked.

Nico blinked, then pulled up the image on his phone. "Yeah, actually." He showed it to Opal. "Like the carving in the tunnel, too. But there was nothing useful down there."

"Not nothing," Tyler countered. "You said the skeleton wore a Nantes Timber uniform?"

Nico nodded, his Logan suspicions flaring anew. Tyler rubbed his chin. "If this poor guy worked at the mill, there should be documentation."

Emma arched an eyebrow. "I bet we could find it."

"Not us," Opal said, her eyes finding Nico's. "But we know who could."

There was a strained beat, then everyone spoke at once.

"Logan."

22

OPAL

Opal knocked on Logan's front door.

She heard a thump and glanced back over her shoulder. Tyler's head ducked behind the garbage cans where he, Nico, and Emma were hiding. "Real subtle," Opal muttered. The sun dipped behind the oak trees lining Overlook Row, flashing pink and red and gold.

No one answered.

Opal pressed the bell, examining the ornate paint job on Logan's house. Her mother was obsessed with repainting their new place in a "historically accurate" way, so the outside was currently a patchwork of different yellows as she hunted for the perfect shade. One more thing Opal didn't understand.

She touched the colorful siding, thinking of all the people who'd lived there. People who lived until they died, and became skeletons. Opal shivered. She had to find out what happened to that man. Her conscience was eating at her for not calling the sheriff, but there was too much at stake. Reporting the skeleton would reveal the Darkdeep to everyone.

"I guess he's not home," Nico whisper-shouted from the sidewalk. But at that very moment, the door opened and Opal found herself face-to-face with Sylvain Nantes.

"Oh, hi." She'd been hoping for Logan or his mom. "Um, is Logan around?"

"Hi, Opal." Logan's father wore a button-down shirt and dress pants, not his usual flannel and jeans. "Lori and I are on our way to a festival board dinner, but Logan and Lily are inside." He held the door open for her.

"Thanks." Opal prayed her friends would stay hidden.

"They're in the kitchen. Go on back." He called up the stairs. "Honey? It's time to go!"

"Almost ready," answered Mrs. Nantes.

Logan and his younger sister were eating dinner and watching an iPad propped between them. "Hey, Opal," Lily greeted her cheerfully.

"Hi, Lily." Opal saw Logan close his eyes briefly before turning to look at her.

"What do you want?" he said.

"Logan!" Lily looked shocked. "That's rude."

They heard footsteps on the stairs. A moment later Logan's mom stuck her head into the room. "Nice to see you, Opal," she said warmly. "We'll be gone a couple of hours, kids. Finish your homework."

Logan waited until his parents bustled out the door. "What do you want?" he repeated.

"Can I talk to you in private?"

"*Oooh.*" Lily grinned as if witnessing something important. "I'll leave you two alone." She wandered from the room, shooting Opal a backward glance that turned into a wink.

"We have a problem," Opal said once Lily was out of earshot.

"*You* have a problem."

"No, it's a *we* thing." Opal pulled out her phone and showed him the skeleton, zooming in on the Nantes Timber Company logo. Logan stared at the picture, then shrugged. "So what?"

"So what?" Opal's eyes narrowed. "That's a human skeleton in a ditch wearing a Nantes company uniform. Aren't you curious about it?"

Logan finally looked at her. His eyes were shadowed, tormented.

Opal nearly gasped. "Logan, are you okay?"

"No, Opal." His voice shook. "I got sucked through a well into a freezing lake, and then a video-game monster tried to kill me. Except that's impossible. So I'm pretty not okay right now. I'm *freaking out.*"

Opal took a deep breath. "Logan, the pool is real. That creature was . . . something we know about. Sort of. I should have told you."

Something heavy moved behind Logan's eyes. "Told me what?"

"About figments. About the Darkdeep."

"The what?" Logan pushed back in his chair and stood. "There's a name for that . . . that darkness? What are you guys *doing* on that island?"

Opal bit her lip. She had to level with him. "Logan, you're not losing your mind. If you help me now, I promise to tell you everything. No more secrets."

Logan stared at her for a long moment.

Opal held his gaze, worried she'd made a terrible mistake. *I had no choice.*

"Okay," he said finally. "It's a deal."

The main office of the Nantes Timber Company was creepy at night. Opal wasn't the only one who felt it. Tyler and Emma huddled close together. Nico darted glances at every shadow. "This feels like enemy territory," he muttered.

"It is," Logan shot back.

Nico didn't respond. Opal prayed the two of them could behave long enough to complete their mission. She hadn't told the others about her agreement with Logan, and butterflies were playing badminton in her stomach. *They'll understand, right? I had no choice!*

Opal pushed the worry aside. She'd done the right thing. She couldn't sit back and watch Logan lose his mind just to protect a secret. That'd be way too heartless. Like it or not, he was a part of this now.

"We're gonna identify this dude and get out of here before anyone sees us." Logan walked ahead of them down a carpeted hallway. The office was near the edge of Timbers, on the western side of Otter Creek, where most of the land belonged to the timber company. This was Logan's turf and they all knew it.

"Where are we going?" Tyler asked.

"Here." Logan stopped at a door labeled *Human Resources*.

"Human what?" Emma deadpanned.

"It means 'personnel.'" Logan rolled his eyes. "The people who oversee hiring and stuff. This is where the records are kept."

The room was standard boring, with drab furniture and harsh fluorescent lighting. Opal spotted a row of metal filing cabinets beside a giant copy machine.

"So we think the skeleton hasn't been there *too* long," Emma said, "because the jacket is old-school, but not, like, vintage." She blew her bangs out of her face. "Like, my mom might've worn it, but not Marilyn Monroe."

"Here." Logan pulled an album down and slapped it open on the table. "The Christmas banquet happens every year. Employees wear their jackets for the group photo."

"Except your dad." Tyler pointed to a picture dated five years before. Sylvain Nantes was in a bright red Santa suit.

Logan's ears turned red. "That was just one year. The regular guy got sick."

There were hundreds of people in the older pictures. "Did your dad invite everyone who worked here?" Opal asked.

"Still does," Logan said proudly. "It's tradition. My grandfather did it that way, too."

"My mom always loved the food," Tyler added. Everyone turned to look at him. "What? She worked here for a while before my sister was born."

Emma tapped one of the photos. "Seems like *everyone* did. Before the layoffs."

The room went still. Opal swore she heard an owl hooting in the distance.

"Everyone loves the banquet," Logan said roughly, flipping through the album. "Nobody misses it, not unless they're on their deathbed or something."

"Wait!" Emma caught a page with her finger. "These jackets look right, and the caption lists everyone's name in the picture. This could really help!"

A vein pumped in Logan's neck. "How do I know that skeleton is real?"

"Because we showed you five pictures of it." Emma waved her phone.

"You could've dressed up a Halloween decoration." His voice was thick with suspicion. "You could be playing me right now."

Acting on instinct, Opal grabbed his hand.

"Your fingers are trembling," Logan said, surprised. He didn't jerk away.

"Because I'm *scared*, Logan." She let go and looked at the others. "We all are. This isn't a joke."

Emma nodded. Tyler dipped his chin in assent. Even Nico muttered, "It's true."

Logan's lips tightened. His gaze shifted to a point beyond Opal, as if he were arguing inside his head. Then he exhaled slowly, some of the tension leaving his shoulders. "Okay. What should we do next?"

"Let's look up these jacket people," Emma said. "Maybe one went missing."

"Fine. But only Opal and I touch the files. Everything has to go back exactly like it was."

"Sounds good to me," Nico joked. "I wouldn't want to leave any fingerprints."

"Your fingerprints are all over this place," Logan snarled. "You and your dad's."

Nico's head dropped. Emma put a hand on his arm.

"And *away* we go," Tyler mumbled under his breath.

———————

Opal had to hand it to the HR department—they kept excellent records. Each file had a picture clipped to it. Logan and Opal had gone through twenty or so when they found a folder that also held an unsealed envelope. "Okay if I open this?" she asked.

He nodded grudgingly. Inside were two paychecks and a note:

Unclaimed personal item stored in section 318-B of company warehouse.

"Does your dad let employees store personal stuff?" Tyler asked.

"Sometimes, yeah."

Opal scanned the file. "Hey, listen! This guy? His name was Roman Hale." She pointed to a notation on the first page. "Get this! Fifteen years ago, a falling tree clipped him while on the job. He refused medical treatment, so they made him sign a waiver."

Tyler snapped his fingers. "Our skeleton has a busted collarbone."

"No home address," Opal murmured. "Only a PO box. No emergency contact, either."

"Maybe he didn't have family," Tyler guessed. "He died alone, outside of the town, and nobody looked hard enough to find him."

"He quit showing up for work." Opal was still reading. "They terminated him after two weeks."

"Our skeleton is definitely terminated," Tyler said.

Emma punched him in the shoulder. "Hey, be respectful."

Tyler grimaced. "Sorry."

Emma pushed the man's photograph to the center of the table.

Weather-beaten face. Bright blue eyes. Dark hair. He had a nice smile.

Opal felt suddenly, overwhelmingly sad.

"Roman Hale," she whispered. "What happened to you?"

23

NICO

Logan squared his shoulders.

"Okay." He faced the others, pushing up his sleeves. "I did my part, and we figured out who the skeleton was. Now I want proof."

Nico crossed his arms. "Proof of what?"

Opal cleared her throat, drawing the spotlight. "I promised Logan that if he helped us, we'd tell him everything we know about figments." She spat the next words quickly. "And the Darkdeep."

"You did what?" Nico shook his head in disbelief. Tyler closed his eyes, and Emma covered her mouth.

Opal spoke in a low, firm voice. "It was the only way to get him to help. Plus, Logan was *attacked* by a figment. It wouldn't be right not to explain. It'd be cruel." She caught Nico's eye and held it. "He thought he was losing it. Can you imagine if you went through the Darkdeep and didn't know what happened?"

A resigned expression stole over Nico's face. "You're right. Done is done."

"Thanks for your approval," Logan said sarcastically. "Now *explain*. What is that vortex? Tell me you guys aren't jumping into it for fun."

Emma winced, then coughed into a fist. Opal glanced at the ceiling while Tyler started whistling tunelessly. Nico had the good grace to blush.

Logan shook his head. "Unbelievable."

"It *is* unbelievable," Emma said. "At first it was fun. We created *amazing* things. Then . . . well . . . it stopped being fun. Now we don't know what to think about it."

Logan held up a hand. "Start from the beginning."

Opal did. Step by step, she walked Logan through what they'd discovered in Still Cove. The cave. The island. The houseboat. The swirling pool down in a basement that shouldn't exist. Logan already knew about the tunnel, and he'd run like a jackrabbit from the robot ogre, but the truth about figments took his breath away. When Opal finished, he sat down heavily in a folding chair, staring at nothing.

Nico actually felt a little sorry for him. "It's a lot to absorb at once."

Logan's head jerked up. "I want to see it."

Nico frowned. "You already did. Volg-Mordan nearly chopped us to pieces."

"Not a figment. I want to see the Darkdeep again."

179

Opal cringed. "We agreed on no more tests until we figure out how it really works."

"I don't want to go *in* the thing." Logan actually shivered. "You guys are insane for doing that. I . . . I just need to see it again. To prove to myself that it's real." His voice cracked slightly. "Please. It's important."

Nico glanced at Opal, who nodded, as did Tyler and Emma.

"Fine, Logan." Nico slapped his hands together. "Fair is fair. We'll go tonight."

"What is going on?" Opal whispered.

They were standing on the ridge, not far from where they'd encountered the rhino. It had taken a few hours for everyone to check in at home and sneak away again. The cove was bitterly cold, with only the moon and their phone lights to see by. Nico had expected to find the island empty. It wasn't.

Down by the pond, the place was lit up like a dance party.

"How many do you see?" Tyler stared at the twinkling lights. "I count six figments near the water alone. They look like trolls holding torches."

"Three stormtroopers ran into the woods." Emma pointed to the dark forest. "They're whacking trees with lightsabers. And there's some kind of sparkling blob stuck in the creek."

"Oh, good gravy." Tyler pressed a fist to his chin. "By the entry stones—is that a glow-in-the-dark gummy bear? Bouncing here and there and everywhere?"

Logan turned incredulous eyes on Opal. "These things show up all the time, and you guys just hang out here?"

"Before now, they only appeared when someone went into the pool." She shot a worried glance at Nico. "We have a serious problem."

Nico ran a hand through his hair. "Emma's right—they're happening on their own now. How can we even get down there?"

Logan straightened. "We're not quitting. I still want to see the Darkdeep."

Nico chewed the inside of his cheek, thinking. "If we swing around behind the houseboat, I think the way is clear. Hopefully the gummy bear will move off before we reach the stepping-stones." Volg/Mordan had broken the first rock, but it split down the middle and a decent-size piece still poked above the water's surface.

"We should hurry." Tyler started down off the ridge. "I feel like a cheeseburger out here, just waiting for something to come take a bite."

They moved carefully, hiding once to avoid a herd of shambling zombies. It took ten long minutes to circle to the far side of the pond. They sprinted across the stones and Nico shut the front door behind them, sinking to the floor in relief.

"Note to anyone thinking imaginary creatures would be cool in real life," he panted. "They're one hundred percent not."

Logan offered him a hand up. Nico stared at it a moment, then took it.

"The pool," Logan said.

Nico nodded. "Let's go." He led everyone through the curtain, across the display room, past the jar thing—were those nostrils in its head now?—and into the secret stairwell. The moment his shoe touched the steps, Nico could tell something had changed.

Eerie lights played on the walls, washed-out colors flashing in discordant bursts. At the bottom Nico saw the Darkdeep itself, and his jaw dropped. The water whirled and churned at breakneck speed, sloshing up into the air without a drop touching the floor.

"It's gone crazy," Opal whispered behind him.

"Like a washing machine on steroids," Tyler said.

Emma shook her head slowly. "Even I'm not getting in *that*."

Logan moved closer, eyes wide as Frisbees. "It's real. I can't believe it. I'd almost convinced myself it was a dream." He started to reach out, then snatched his fingers back.

Nico rubbed his forehead. "It's clearly overloading, but how can we make it stop?"

Opal lifted her chin. "We'll keep researching. Every minute matters now. Two days ago, this island was under control.

Now it's a monster convention. Who knows what tomorrow might be like?"

Something crashed upstairs. All eyes shot to the staircase.

Heavy treads crossed the deck above their heads.

Tyler leaped to Nico's side and whispered into his ear. "*Something's inside the boat!*"

"*I can tell*," Nico hissed back. When no one else moved, he threw his hands up. "Fine. Stay here." But as he stepped toward the stairs, Logan put a hand on his shoulder. "I'll go with you," he said.

Nico nodded gratefully. "Just be ready to run back down here."

They crept up the steps. There was another crash, followed by peculiar grunting. Nico's palms began to sweat. He eased open the wall panel and poked his nose out.

Nico froze. His heart stopped beating.

Not ten paces from where he hid, three orcs were fighting over the pirate sword.

"What is it?" Logan whispered. "Is something there?"

Nico shook a hand at him for quiet. But when he looked back into the room, the center orc was staring right at him. "Oh no," Nico breathed.

The orc roared. It dropped the sword and pointed.

"Get back!" Nico shouted, jerking the panel shut. Searching frantically, he spotted a deadbolt on the inside of the wall. Nico slammed it home with a grateful moan, then pushed Logan back down the stairs. Fists began hammering from the opposite side, but the bolt held.

Nico jumped the last few steps to the floorboards. "We've got trouble! There are freaking orcs upstairs and they know we're here." The banging above underscored his warning.

"What do we do?" Tyler squealed. "There's no other way out!"

Nico swallowed. "There's one other way." He glanced at the seething, spiraling pool.

Opal's eyes nearly popped from her head. "Are you *kidding*?"

"What choice do we have?!"

Splintering sounds above. Time was running out.

"It's okay," Emma said, voice trembling. "We've done it before. I'll go first." She turned to the vortex, all color draining from her face. "Best not to think too long." With a yelp of fright, Emma launched herself into the pool.

The Darkdeep froze, pulsed once, then spasmed in a fiery bloom.

It took several seconds for Nico's vision to clear. "Who's next?" he shouted.

Tyler growled deep in his throat. "Not cool, man!" Squeezing his eyes shut, he threw himself into the raging water.

Nico felt a lurch like a record skipping. Tyler was gone.

Nico could see the whites of Logan's eyes. *He's not ready for this.* If Logan went in totally panicked, what would happen? What would the Darkdeep read? "Opal, you're next."

Something cracked overhead. A spine-tingling roar boomed into the chamber.

"No more time." Nico felt a sudden, strange calm. "Opal, go on."

Opal glanced from one boy to the other. "You two better be right behind me!" She dove into the water and disappeared. The pool shuddered, then whirled like a tornado.

Logan was staring at the Darkdeep with a look of horror on his face. His gaze snapped to Nico. "You go next. I . . . I'll be last." Nico saw that his hands were shaking badly.

"Sure thing." Nico put a hand on Logan's shoulder. Felt the tension of his muscles. "Just be sure not to hit the drain-pipe on the way down."

Logan gave him a wild look. "Drainpipe?"

Heavy feet slammed onto the stairs.

"Yeah, that one." Nico pointed into the whirlpool.

Logan leaned forward to see.

Nico shoved him in the back with both hands and watched Logan plunge shrieking into the inky black depths.

A murderous snarl. Hot orc breath on Nico's neck.

Nico hurled himself after Logan with a wail of pure terror.

"*Psst*, over here!"

Nico's eyes snapped open. He shook his waterlogged head. He'd gone through the Darkdeep. They all had. Which meant they should be outside in the pond. He tried to remember what the trip had felt like, and discovered he couldn't. Where the memory should be was only . . . static. Fuzz and white noise.

Opal reached down and tugged Nico's shirt. "Come on," she whispered. "It's not safe." She gathered him into a sprint for the tunnel entrance.

At the foot of the rise, Nico spotted Emma, Tyler, and a fuming Logan Nantes.

"We're gonna talk about that shove," Logan said darkly, water coating his hair.

"Whatever." Nico felt only relief at seeing them all alive. "Let's get off this island."

They stole to the tunnel mouth, encountering zero figments along the way. Nico was about to relax when Opal gasped, a hand shooting to her mouth.

He edged forward. "Opal, what is it?"

She didn't answer, pointing at the soft mud in front of the tunnel.

Massive footprints led inside.

They didn't come back out.

24
OPAL

*F*aster. *Faster.*

Opal and Nico propelled the rowboat across the murky water.

She had to get away. From the figments, the houseboat, the Darkdeep, all of it.

They'd abandoned the tunnel entrance and snuck across the island instead. No way was Opal going into the passage. Not with those footprints disappearing inside. The idea of meeting a figment down in the dark underneath the cove was too horrible to contemplate.

Opal's oar struck something and a twisted metal object bobbed to the surface. At first she worried she'd hit some new Darkdeepian creature, but then she recognized it. "Nico. Your drone."

Emma clicked her tongue. Logan's face was stricken.

"I think I can reach." Opal extended her paddle toward the mangled quadcopter.

"Forget it," Nico hissed. "It's wrecked. Worry about whatever dredged it up from the bottom."

Tyler's voice trembled. "You think—you think it could be the Beast?"

A splash sounded behind them. *Just a fish*, Opal told herself. *A huge jumping fish. It's fine.*

"You *do* worry about the Beast a lot," Emma whispered. "And the Darkdeep reads minds."

"Oh no." Tyler slumped into the belly of the rowboat. "Please, anything but that."

"Relax," Opal said, trying to sound convincing. "We're off the island. Whatever figments we just made will have to enjoy their lifespans without us."

"But *something* left," Tyler shot back, his voice unsteady. "You saw the tracks."

"I'm sure it can't go far." Opal pulled back on her oar, fighting off the shakes. "I bet it just went a little way down the tunnel and now it's stuck. Maybe—"

The boat jolted. Opal almost lost her paddle, catching it a split second before it flopped into the water. They'd hit an old sailboat, covered in seaweed and floating upside down like a bloated fish. Opal could barely read the name painted on its side: *Roman Holiday*.

"Roman," Emma breathed. "That was his first name. The man who died."

Debris began floating to the surface all around them.

Tangles of netting, a rusted lantern, bits of metal and wood, a picked-clean bone. The last looked anything but human.

"Faster!" Opal said out loud.

Nico needed no encouragement. Together they pulled for the cave as quickly as possible.

With shaking fingers, Opal helped Nico tie off the rowboat. The group scurried up the cliff notches in a mad scramble to get clear of the water. Gathering on the ledge, they eyed the cave mouth, ready to bolt at the slightest noise.

"Do you think it came all the way through?" Logan asked, voice low.

"Let's not stay and find out," Emma whispered back.

Phone light blazing, Nico pointed up the path. "Let's get our bikes. Be careful climbing in the dark. No one wants to fall, believe me."

Logan didn't move. "Then what?"

"I don't know." Opal glanced at the silent, glowering cave. "But I don't want to sit here thinking it over."

"Me neither." Emma started up the path, Tyler and Logan on her heels. Opal was about to follow when she heard a huge splash below the ledge. Wood cracked and splintered.

"The boat," Nico hissed. "Something's destroying it!"

"Go!" Opal whispered. "Now!"

The group raced to the top, not daring to look back. Opal

grabbed her bike and switched on its headlight. Could they out-pedal whatever might be chasing them? She led out, pumping her feet furiously. Before she'd gone twenty yards, Opal spotted deep scores in the grass.

Torn earth. Mangled bushes. Snapped branches. Opal rode along a trail of destruction aimed directly at Timbers.

She thought of the footprints in the mud.

Something left the island ahead of us.

Where was it now?

Opal's tires slid out. She crashed sideways, her elbow and knee taking the brunt of the fall. Opal gritted her teeth as the others skidded to a stop. Emma dismounted and crouched beside her. "Are you all right?"

"I think so." Opal felt dazed and sharpened at the same time. Her body throbbed, and she was wet from whatever she'd landed on.

Nico, Logan, and Tyler walked their bikes closer.

"What *is* that stuff?" Logan said.

"Huh?" Opal clicked on her phone light.

A silver ooze coated the ground. Opal was covered in it.

"Careful." Opal watched as blood from her knee mixed with the silvery muck. "No one touch me until we know what we're dealing with."

"But you're hurt." Emma's fingers flexed uselessly. "That slime is all over you."

Opal stumbled to her feet. "I'm okay. I can ride." She felt

blood trickle down her elbow. She knew it was blood because it felt nice and warm. Was it weird that her blood felt nice? *Did I hit my head?*

"I'll take the lead," Nico said. The others surrounded Opal, letting her ride in the middle. Her bike creaked and groaned. She dripped bloody ooze onto the grass.

"Almost there," Logan called from behind her.

"You got this," Tyler added.

They topped the last hill overlooking Main Street. Opal glanced left at Overlook Row. She could go home, curl up in bed, and pretend none of this ever happened.

But beneath the streetlights downtown, Opal saw strange shapes gathering.

One growled, dropping to all fours.

Another hissed darkly, a sibilant, seeking sound.

Opal smelled something decayed. Her skin tingled with static electricity.

The largest shadow reached up a huge, hairy arm. Teeth flashed yellow-white in the moonlight as it gripped a radish festival banner and tore it down, the fabric crumpling like an autumn leaf.

Opal accepted the awful truth.

Figments had invaded Timbers.

PART FOUR

THE DARKDEEP

25

NICO

We're in trouble," Nico breathed.

The figments had gathered at the heart of sleeping Timbers. Nico had no idea what would happen if anyone walked by on a late-night stroll. There was no explaining *this* away.

In a single glance Nico spotted a werewolf, a Sasquatch, a Power Ranger, some sort of silver-oozing snake-man, and a floating, wispy fairy. How had they escaped the island? *How are we supposed to stop them?*

Nico and the others stood with their bikes on the hill overlooking town. Tyler pressed a palm to his forehead. "Okay, this is officially above our pay grade. Let's call Sheriff Ritchie."

"And tell him what?" Nico countered. "That imaginary beings are trashing town square?"

"Nico, *what else can we do?*" Tyler pointed in exasperation. "There's a freaking monster riot on Main Street."

"The sheriff's office is two towns over." Emma hugged her

body tight. "These creatures might disappear before the deputies arrive, and then we'd be busted for pranking."

"Pranking?" Logan let his bike drop to the dirt. "Those things are destroying the park!"

It was true. The Sasquatch walked to a bench and kicked it over, then sniffed the underside. The snake-man had slithered into the fountain, oozing silver all over the stonework. The werewolf tossed its head and unleashed a piercing howl, which set dogs barking a dozen blocks away.

Nico's heart pounded. He'd always feared werewolves, but did this one spring from *his* mind? Or had someone else created it? If so, *how*?

"Did we make these?" Emma asked quietly. "When we all went in together?"

"Maybe." Opal set her own bike down. "It doesn't matter. We need to lure them away somehow. We can't let anyone else see this, or everything is ruined."

"Lure them away." Tyler stared at Opal, speaking in a flat voice. "As in, intentionally get their attention, in hopes that they'll chase us."

"They're destroying the festival decorations! It's supposed to start tomorrow."

Nico watched the chaos with sick fascination. The Power Ranger was methodically side-kicking a stage support, causing the whole structure to slump. The fairy was zipping around in circles, wand-blasting the statue of Timbers' founder, Edward Nantes.

Opal seemed ready to burst. "This is our fault. *We* have to fix it."

Nico scratched his cheek, thinking furiously. "I'll ride straight through the group of figments, then cut back toward the hills. Maybe they'll follow me."

Logan scoffed. "That might get one or two, but all of them? We need something bigger."

Emma's face lit up. "The festival is planning fireworks, right?"

Logan nodded. "Compliments of Nantes Timber Company."

"Then they must be here already." Emma grabbed Nico's arm. "We could send a couple of riders to get the figments' attention. Then someone could set rockets off up here to draw them out of town."

"I know where the fireworks are!" Opal pointed at the stage. The fairy floated close beside it, tittering gleefully as the Power Ranger continued whacking at supports. "They're in a storage container behind the stage. I heard Mr. Murphy telling my mom the other day!"

"It'll be locked," Nico pointed out. "They're not going to leave fireworks lying around where anyone could get to them."

"It might not be," Opal said hopefully. "This *is* Timbers."

"Great." Tyler hung his head in resignation. "So we need a distraction to get our hands on the distraction."

"I have an idea." Logan glanced at Nico. "How much time do we have?"

Nico shrugged helplessly. "Until someone wakes up and notices a team of monsters demolishing the downtown. Why?"

Logan ignored him and turned to Opal. "I need your help. Come on."

———————

Nico cringed at all the noise the figments were making. He, Tyler, and Emma were in an alley twenty yards away from town square. The creatures were still occupied with breaking things and pulling radish signs down from street posts—or, in the Sasquatch's case, pulling down the street posts themselves. Nico worried the sound might carry to the residential streets a few blocks away.

"This is nuts," Tyler whispered. "Look at them!"

The Power Ranger and the snake-man had started wrestling in the fountain. The fairy was now using its wand to split things in half, like a fire hydrant, which had earned the figment an unexpected dousing.

"What's taking so long?" Nico grumbled for the third time.

Tyler lifted his palms to the sky.

"I cannot *believe* I can't film this," Emma muttered, pacing in nervous circles. "Hollywood has nothing on the Darkdeep. I'd be world famous as a special effects master."

"Until you had to explain how it worked," Tyler said.

Nico heard the purr of an engine. He spun to see two sets

of headlights approaching at a slow roll. Logan popped off the lead ATV. "Okay, we're ready," he called.

"Took you long enough," Nico grumbled, but low and to himself. Was he jealous Opal got to ride the other four-wheeler? Maybe a little.

"Everyone clear on the plan?" Logan asked. Though it was hard to see in the headlights' glare, Nico thought he heard a smile in Logan's voice. *He's looking forward to this.*

Logan hoisted a bolt cutter. "I brought this just in case."

"Good idea." Nico said. He and Emma picked up their bikes. Tyler hopped on the second four-wheeler behind Opal. "I like calm, smooth rides," he whispered. "Remember that turtles win all the races."

Opal reached back and patted his leg. "Those aren't rabbits out there, Ty."

"Don't be late," Nico warned, voice firm.

"Don't be slow." Logan slapped down his visor.

Nico didn't bother to respond. He thrust a fist out at Emma, who bumped it with her own. "You sure you want to do this?" Nico asked.

Emma surprised him by laughing. "Um, *yeah*. When will I get to be monster bait again?"

Nico chuckled. "That's one way of looking at it."

They pedaled around the corner, then silently sped toward town square.

The Sasquatch saw them first. It was sitting on the

sidewalk, pounding a mailbox into a metal pancake as Nico rolled by. "Hey, Harry. How's the weather?"

The Sasquatch roared and stood, lumbering after them. Nico and Emma picked up speed, popping onto the sidewalk that bordered the square. Emma blew a kiss at the snake-man. It dropped the Power Ranger and started to follow, but Nico and Emma reached the next corner and turned, racing toward the stage.

"Keep moving!" Nico shouted. They passed behind the platform, drawing a squeal from the fairy and a growl from the werewolf. The fairy's glowing eyes narrowed. Something sizzled past Nico's ear. A bush in front of him burst into cinders.

"Tinker Bell is shooting at us!" Emma yelled. She was glued to Nico's back tire as they tore down to the next corner and turned again, completing half the circuit.

Nico glanced back. The snake-man and werewolf were chasing them, but the fairy had lost interest. It kept lighting more bushes on fire. The Power Ranger charged ahead to cut them off before they could turn again.

"Stop!" Nico slammed on his brakes. Emma jerked to a halt beside him. "We won't make it all the way around. Hang tight a second."

Nico tried not to panic as the figments converged. Then he heard rumbling engines as the ATVs rolled behind the stage with their lights doused. Three shadows dragged a box from the storage container and began lashing it to the lead four-wheeler. *Come on come on come on.*

"Nico," Emma said in a trembling voice. "I think we'd better go."

Emma was right. The Power Ranger stalked toward them along the sidewalk, while the snake-man and werewolf were coming across the grass. The murderous fairy whizzed in from the other side, its tiny wand sparkling with menace.

"New plan," Nico blurted. "We go down the middle and pedal for the hills."

The ATVs drove off. The Power Ranger was less than ten yards away and closing.

"Now, Emma!" They shot forward like corks from a champagne bottle, hurtling directly through the park. *We can shoot the gap between Werewolf and Snake-man. We can make it!*

Emma pedaled feverishly beside Nico. The werewolf howled and leaped, its claws swiping an inch from Nico's throat. Emma ducked under the snake-man's lashing bite and suddenly they were through. Snarling, the figments spun and gave chase.

Nico smiled fiercely. They'd done it! They'd broken free *and* gotten the creatures' attention. He slowed to a coast, reveling in the taste of victory.

But he'd forgotten about Bigfoot.

The Sasquatch stepped directly into their path, causing

both bikes to swerve. Emma kept upright and managed to shoot past, but Nico toppled over the curb and crashed.

"Nico!" Emma started to brake. Nico rolled to his feet and waved her onward.

"Go!" he shouted. "Set off the fireworks!"

Emma began pumping her feet twice as hard. "We'll distract them. Hold on!"

Nico spun to find the Sasquatch glaring down at him with intelligent eyes. It picked up Nico's bike and tossed it aside, thundering a roar. Then the figment stomped the pavement, chest heaving, giant hands flexing in what seemed like frustration.

Nico felt an odd tug at his heart. Though huge and terrifying, the creature carried a nobility its anger couldn't mask. The Sasquatch glanced back at the other figments, who were racing closer by the second, and let out another growl.

It's confused. It doesn't belong here.

Nico wished the Sasquatch hadn't been conjured to this dark street. *It should be roaming the hills like in the legends*, he thought. *Not trapped in a place it doesn't understand.*

Nico felt sorry for it.

The creature tilted its head, then stepped forward and grabbed Nico by his sweatshirt, lifting him to eye level. Nico couldn't breathe. He reached out a shaking hand and patted the Sasquatch's wrist. "S-sorry, big guy. Please d-don't kill me."

Bigfoot vanished. Nico dropped to the pavement like a water balloon.

He shook his head, unable to believe his luck. The figment had disappeared an instant before it could kill him. Or had *he* done something? If so, Nico couldn't say what. Another howl split the night, driving everything else from his brain. Nico ran for his bike, mounted, and pushed away just as the other figments arrived.

In the sky above the hill, red-and-white starbursts exploded, lighting up the night. The remaining figments stopped as if poleaxed, then rushed toward the fireworks, ignoring Nico as he swerved down a side street and pedaled away.

As windows opened and doors slammed, with shouts of "Fire!" carrying up the block, Nico coasted away from the anarchy on Main Street.

He'd done enough for one night.

26
OPAL

It's aftermath," Opal said softly. "Aftermath *everywhere*."

She picked up a radish banner. The grinning vegetable was torn in half. Deep furrows crisscrossed the square's formerly manicured lawn. The stage sagged in the middle. Bent and broken lampposts littered the block.

Townspeople walked around in a daze. Mr. Murphy stood by the fountain, head bowed as he surveyed the damage. Principal Kisner was sweeping up pools of broken glass.

"Who would do this?" Opal's mother asked, a catch in her voice.

Opal didn't answer. *What* would do this was the real question. She glanced at the muddy ATV tracks leading into the hills. Could they trace those back to Logan?

"It's awful," Opal said, and meant it. Even though the festival was super cheesy, people had worked hard on it. And in a blink, overnight, everything had been ruined.

"*Vandals*," Mrs. Walsh spat, scowling at a crumpled stop sign. "With some kind of heavy equipment to steal the fireworks." She glanced at Opal. "You said you were with friends after school yesterday."

"Uh-huh." Opal began to sweat. What if her mom discovered she'd snuck out?

"Who were they? Do I know their parents?"

"Just some kids from school," Opal said quickly. "One of them was Logan."

For the first time, his name didn't make her mother smile. Mrs. Walsh examined the bike tracks running down the sidewalk. "What were you doing?"

"Practicing our talents. There's still going to be a pageant, right?"

"I don't know." Mrs. Walsh's voice broke. Her gaze shifted to Mr. Murphy. She walked over to the old man, putting a hand on his shoulder and leaning in to say something.

"*Psst*. Opal!"

Opal looked behind her. Nico, Emma, Tyler, and Logan were bunched next to the battered stage. Emma waved her over. "*Come on.*"

Opal shot a quick glance at her mom before hurrying to join her friends. "What's up?"

"My movie debut got cancelled," Emma said glumly. "The projection equipment is smashed, and that's gonna cost a fortune."

"All this carnage is expensive," Tyler said. "I bet they have to cancel the festival now. They're not gonna spend money on new radish banners when the streetlights need fixing."

"Can we imagine gold coins inside the Darkdeep?" Emma suggested. "That'd solve a lot of problems."

"Until they all disappeared," Nico reminded her. "What good would that do?"

"I don't think it would work anyway." Tyler shoved his hands in his pockets. "Inanimate objects haven't come out of the Darkdeep. Even that chicken nugget was rolling around."

"The figments were definitely animate last night." Opal shuddered. "And they lasted forever. I wish there was some trick to make them disappear."

"Yeah, about that." Nico scuffed his shoe on the pavement. "I might've done something to make the Sasquatch vanish."

"What?" the others blurted in unison. It would have been funny if everything weren't such a mess.

"When Bigfoot picked me up, I . . . I talked to it." He shrugged self-consciously. "I said I was sorry and asked it not to kill me."

"So you begged for your life." Logan snorted derisively. "What, you think it felt bad for you and dissolved itself out of pity?"

Opal cringed, but Nico didn't take the bait.

"No, not like that." He chewed his bottom lip, his eyes getting a faraway look. "I felt something . . . change. I wasn't afraid for a second. Up close like that, I could see how much the Sasquatch didn't belong there."

No one spoke. The wind whipped shredded strips of canvas across the mangled grass.

"So we just, like . . . apologize?" Tyler said finally. "To the figments?"

Nico's features bunched as he shook his head. "No, that's not it. But . . . I don't know."

"We bring the figments into being," Emma said. "It makes sense you connected with one."

Logan crossed his arms. "What are you saying? We should tell these monsters we love them?"

"Be serious, Logan." Opal pressed her hands together, thinking. "Maybe it was the way you looked at the Sasquatch, Nico. How you really *saw* it."

Tyler grunted. "We're supposed to have staring contests?"

"*No*," Opal snapped, growing frustrated. "I just meant that Nico paying closer attention to the problem might be part of the solution."

"If he did anything at all," Logan muttered.

Rain spattered across town square, but no one moved. The weather matched their mood.

Emma shivered. "The bigger question is, how'd they escape? I thought figments couldn't leave the island."

"And where are they all coming from?" Tyler added with a frown. "We might've created last night's monster squad by diving in to avoid those orcs, but there were dozens of figments on the island when we got there. If *we* didn't make them, who did?"

"Maybe the Darkdeep doesn't need us anymore," Emma whispered.

A squeal of feedback reverberated across the square. Everyone jumped.

"This is Mayor Hayt," a female voice boomed from the lone undamaged stage speaker. "I want you all to know I'm doing everything in my power to determine the cause of this criminality. The perpetrators *will* be caught and held accountable. And we *will* hold our wonderful radish festival, as soon as possible."

A faint cheer went up from the crowd, but Opal's heart sank. The last thing they needed was an official investigation with the Darkdeep running wild.

"I need your cooperation in two crucial ways," Mayor Hayt continued. "First, if you have any information about this atrocity, please come forward to the authorities. A substantial reward is being offered courtesy of the Nantes Timber Company."

There was a muted round of applause. Mayor Hayt waited a beat. "Second, we need to let our cleanup crew get started. So please clear the square, and be sure to attend to your festival duties. We'll get this straightened out. Thank you."

Another feedback screech, and the mayor's voice was gone.

"We're the perpetrators she's talking about," Tyler groaned.

Emma punched his arm. "Figments did this, not us. We *stopped* the destruction."

"Whatever helps you sleep." Tyler rubbed the spot she'd hit. "But we definitely have information."

"Not enough." Emma took out her phone and scrolled through more blank photos. "We don't have any evidence. If we say a bunch of imaginary creatures rampaged through downtown, they'll think we're lying. Or commit us to an insane asylum."

"Or think we did it." Logan's cheek twitched. "I saw Sheriff Ritchie photographing the ATV tracks. Not many people around here have Trailbreaker Extremes."

Emma giggled. "Your dad's going to flip out if he has to reward someone for turning his son in."

Logan didn't share her amusement.

"We won't let that happen," Opal assured him. "You've got four alibis lined up."

"Unless it's enough for a new quadcopter," Nico muttered, but he smiled to show he was kidding. Logan grinned back sourly.

"Real talk: we could take the mayor to the houseboat right now." Tyler's voice was growing desperate. "Just show her the freaking Darkdeep and get out of this mess. Anyone who sees it will believe everything we say."

No. A voice spoke inside Opal, both foreign and familiar at once. *The Darkdeep must be kept secret.* It felt like ice water sweeping through her veins, but all she said was, "I think taking people there is a very bad idea."

There was a tense silence before the others nodded one by one. Even Tyler. He sighed with his whole body. "So we're back to square zero. Again."

"We still have one clue," Opal said. In her mind, she could see the lonely skeleton at the bottom of the ravine. "We didn't finish looking into Roman Hale."

Emma's eyes widened. "Right! He left something in the timber company's warehouse."

"I'll swipe my dad's keys." Logan shook his head, as if surprised by the words coming out of his mouth. "We can four-wheel out there if I'm not already on the FBI's Most Wanted list."

Tyler exhaled, his cheeks puffing. "Our parents are going to notice we're gone this time. Last night's demolition derby guarantees it."

"No choice," Nico said. "We have to figure this out."

"Going rogue." Emma stuck out her hand. "Let's try this again."

Opal put hers on top of Emma's. Nico's came next, then Tyler. They all looked at Logan.

"Fine," he snarked. "But you guys should know that I'll inform on all of you to lighten my sentence." He shook his head as he placed his hand on top of theirs. "To a life of crime."

"To a teensy *day* of crime," Emma corrected. "To save Timbers."

"*To save Timbers*," they all repeated.

When they broke apart, Opal felt a single word, sung deep within.

Something she knew was *her* thought, *her* want.

Yes.

27

NICO

Nico slammed back against the chain-link fence.

Two Dobermans were charging straight for him, razor-sharp teeth exposed.

So this is how I go out. Chewed to pieces by Nantes Company guard dogs.

Logan dropped onto the gravel next to him and whistled. "Cecil! Peanut! *Heel.*"

The animals slid to a stop, heads tilting in confusion. The lead dog whined and pawed the ground. "Good boys," Logan cooed, and their ears went up. They trotted forward and licked his hand, tails wagging happily.

Nico started breathing again. "A little warning next time," he grumbled.

Logan shot Nico a wink. "Sorry, couldn't resist. Plus, Peanut's all talk, aren't you, boy?" He ruffled the dog's black fur. The animal preened under his attention.

Three more sets of sneakers hit the ground. Tyler. Emma. Opal. The dogs paid no more attention, satisfied by Logan's presence. He sent them off with final head pats. "Let's go. We're lucky the motion sensors are turned off during the day. Those aren't as easy to win over."

Logan led them across the crowded timber yard toward a massive gray warehouse. They crept from piles of felled trees to stacks of treated lumber, zipping around giant bladed machines that could slice Nico in half without a hitch. Reaching the last bit of cover—a large drill lashed to a flatbed truck—they hunkered down and peered at an oversized steel door.

"This is the back entrance," Logan said quietly. "There's usually not much activity in the afternoon, especially around lunch, but if we run into anyone let me do the talking."

Nico held his tongue. Though it sucked having Logan Freaking Nantes running the show, everything he said made sense. Nico had to be a team player. Too much was at stake.

To be fair, he hasn't been as awful lately.

Nico straightened, surprised by the admission. Logan was a sworn enemy. He'd gone out of his way to make Nico's life miserable for almost a year. Nico's whole future in Timbers was in jeopardy because of the Nantes family, yet here the two of them were, huddled shoulder to shoulder, plotting to break into a warehouse together. *Lunacy.*

"You have a map or something?" Tyler shifted uncomfortably. "I don't wanna get lost in there."

Logan gave him a level look. "My family's run this company for four generations. I don't need a map of our own warehouse. Besides, it's not as full as it used to be. Not since . . ." His gaze flicked to Nico, then shot away.

Nico felt his cheeks burn.

"We should hurry," Opal said, changing the subject. "And there's no reason for everyone to go inside." She turned to Tyler and Emma. "Will you two keep watch? I'd hate to get nabbed sneaking back out."

"What if those dogs come back?" Tyler said.

"They won't bother you now," Logan assured him. "They've seen you with me. Plus, I wasn't kidding about them being all talk. Let Peanut sniff your hand and you're fine."

"Easy for you to say," Tyler muttered. "Stick my hand in its mouth? I *like* my fingers."

"We'll climb that." Emma pointed to a gigantic yellow machine tipped by steel claws. "There's an open window, so we can hide inside. Plus, we'll see more if we're higher up."

"Just don't *be* seen," Logan warned. "And don't touch the controls. We'll meet back here in"—Logan glanced skyward as if estimating—"fifteen minutes. If there's trouble, whistle when you see us at the door."

"I can't whistle," Tyler hissed.

Emma slugged his shoulder. "*Come on*. I'll teach you."

They split up, Nico, Logan, and Opal crouch-running to the door. Logan unlocked it and they slipped inside, shutting it firmly behind them.

The warehouse was dim and gloomy, the only light spilling in through dingy windows set up high near the ceiling. Towering rows of shelves flanked a wide central aisle. These held sawed boards and planks of every description, as well as drills, machine parts, and other things Nico couldn't identify. Logan moved confidently, as if he knew what everything was and how it was used. Against his will, Nico's respect for him grew.

Logan strode quickly past row after row. At the far end they reached a sliding wall with a zip-flapped door. "This is where employees can store things," Logan said. "Some lumberjacks don't have anywhere to keep their personal tools, so my dad provides a room for them. Not for valuables or anything, but stuff the workers need."

He opened the door and they stepped inside. This room was smaller, lined with shelves like you might see in a supply closet. The rows were labeled by letter and number. Logan walked to the very back section, where a faded yellow sign read: UNCLAIMED ITEMS.

Logan tapped the sign. "Roman Hale's property would've been moved here after he was fired. Hopefully it's still here. After ten years, unclaimed items are sold at public auction."

"So where would his stuff be?" Nico asked.

Logan rubbed his chin. "You have the number from his file?"

"Yep." Opal whipped out her phone. "Section 318-B."

Logan walked slowly down the aisle, stepping through

shafts of pale sunlight. He stopped halfway and reached up to remove a small grime-covered chest from the top shelf, accidentally dumping a river of dust onto his head in the process.

He set the chest down and sneezed like a machine gun, then hawked onto the concrete floor. "*Gross*. That's definitely been there a while."

Opal knelt and opened it while Logan wiped dirt from his eyes.

There was a latch but no padlock, which disappointed Nico. This wasn't the type of container used to store precious things.

A single cloth-wrapped bundle was nestled inside.

Nico peered down over Opal's shoulder. "What is it?"

She unwrapped the moth-eaten fabric. The three of them stared in silence.

"Huh," Nico said finally.

It was a smooth stone cylinder roughly two feet long and six inches wide. Opal lifted it in her hands, spinning the object to examine it. "Heavy," she murmured.

Logan straightened with an irritated grunt. "Well, that's disappointing."

Nico had to agree. This was a useless piece of rock.

"Wait!" Opal caught a sunbeam on its weathered surface. "There's an engraving. Some kind of dull image." She traced the pattern with a finger. "It's the hand torch!"

"From the tunnel!" Nico agreed. "And the necklaces."

Opal smacked her head. "We haven't paid enough attention to that."

"We've been a little busy," Nico reminded her.

"What's going on?" Logan glanced back and forth, not enjoying being left out.

"This symbol is carved into the floor of the tunnel," Opal explained, her voice growing excited. "It's also on the necklace we found on Hale's skeleton, and in some houseboat pictures, too. The image ties him to the island. And the Darkdeep, probably!"

Logan frowned. "But this stone thing is useless."

"Wait." Opal angled the cylinder and squinted. "There's writing! But it's not in English. '*Accipere Victus.*' Anyone understand that?"

"Latin?" Nico guessed. "Greek?"

Opal and Logan both shrugged.

Opal continued to rotate the artifact in her hands. "There's a tiny crack," she murmured, "right here, in the center . . ." She pressed a fingernail into it, and a thin line appeared. Opal chewed her lip, thinking. Then she gripped both ends and spun them in opposite directions.

The cylinder divided in half.

"*Bingo.* It's a tube." She eased the sections apart.

Another object slid out, but Nico caught it. "Whoa," he said. "Good thing it fell handle first."

He was holding some kind of antique dagger. The blade was long and thin, sharpened on both sides and ending in a wicked point like an ice pick. It had an odd double guard, and the hilt was carved with the same torch insignia.

"*Not* cool," Logan said. "Workers aren't allowed to store weapons in here."

"But what's it for?" Nico hefted the knife. "Why hide an ancient dagger in a stone tube?"

Logan waved a hand vaguely. "To . . . you know . . . fight things." Then his eyes widened. "Maybe we can use it against the figments!"

"Can I hold it?" Opal asked. Nico handed her the dagger. She flipped it upside down and ran a finger along the tarnished handle. The bottom of the hilt stuck out oddly, and was notched and serrated in a bizarre pattern. Opal suddenly squealed. "Nico, this part looks like a key!"

"Jeez, it could be." Nico blinked. "Maybe we should go back to the tunnel. The carving is in that weird open space, and we've never really looked around."

Opal nodded, eyes shining. "We definitely could've missed something."

Logan ran a hand through his dust-caked hair. "The tunnel? With those *things* roaming through there? That doesn't sound like a great idea."

Nico met Logan's eye squarely. "What's happening is our fault, Logan. Me, Opal, Tyler, and Emma. We started this. If there's a way to stop the Darkdeep, it's our responsibility to find it and shut it down."

Logan's eyelid twitched. His fingers trembled slightly.

"But *you* didn't start anything," Nico continued. "This is *our* mess. None of us will think less of you if you bail. But I think Timbers is in serious danger, including this warehouse, your dad's company, our homes, everything."

Logan's jaw clenched. Something clouded his eyes.

"I'm sorry about your quadcopter," he said suddenly.

Nico gawked.

"I never said it to you, but I am." Logan spoke in an even voice, but the intensity of his gaze pinned Nico to the floor. "And I'm gonna tell my dad to leave yours alone. I don't know if he will, but . . . what's happening isn't right. Your dad was just doing his job."

Logan glanced at Opal, who stared back at him.

Nico realized his mouth was still hanging open. He closed it. Swallowed. There was an awkward silence.

Logan cleared his throat. "What I'm *saying* is, I'm in. Let's find out what this dagger is for. Let's save our freaking town."

Opal actually clapped her hands. "Awesome!"

A smile broke through on Nico's face.

"Yeah, man. Let's do it."

28
OPAL

So *that's* new," Tyler muttered.

Mist curled up from Still Cove, wraithlike tendrils swirling over the cliffs above the cave, as though a ghostly, limber, writhing forest had grown overnight. Opal reached out to touch a wisp, but it slipped through her fingers.

"Not really." Logan climbed off his four-wheeler. "There's always fog near Still Cove."

Emma shuddered. "Not like this."

"I wonder if the Darkdeep affects it." Opal gripped the dagger tightly, pressing its handle into her palm. She was anxious to reach the tunnel, but her nerves danced, electric with warning.

What's waiting for us?

Massive footprints remained in the grass, but there were no new signs of figments.

"It's quiet," Tyler whispered.

"*Too* quiet," everyone else said at once. They exchanged glances and chuckled uneasily. Emma turned in a slow 360, scanning the empty field. "They were everywhere last night, and now . . . nothing."

Nothing.

The word seemed to echo. The smell of wet stone carried on the breeze.

"What if we'd never brought the quadcopter out here?" Emma wondered aloud.

Nico snorted. "I'd be wearing a radish suit right now."

"I'd never have experienced the joy of unarmed robbery," Tyler mused.

"I wouldn't have gotten to see Godzilla," Emma said dreamily.

Logan gaped at Emma. "Wait, what?"

Opal grinned. "You missed a few parts." Opal realized she found it almost impossible to imagine life before the houseboat. Would they have to destroy the Darkdeep? Was that even possible? *One step at a time.*

"My parents are probably looking for me already," Tyler said.

Logan sighed. "My dad's going to notice the ATVs are gone."

"Right." Opal straightened her shoulders. "We should get going."

But no one moved, not even Opal. A strange tension

221

paralyzed her, as if her subconscious mind was rebelling against entering the fog. Then she heard a curious sound.

A slow, methodical clicking echoed up from the cove.

"Guys?" Nico's voice shook. "You hear that?"

"Sounds like chopsticks," Tyler hissed. "It's coming from the path."

"No." Opal watched the mist roil. "Not the path. The cliff."

The fog parted as a giant shape dragged itself over the edge of the bluff. Logan staggered backward in alarm. "What the heck is that?!"

It took Opal's mind a beat to accept what she was seeing.

Black-brown body. Clacking mandibles. Dark, enormous eyes.

"Oh no," Emma whispered, her face draining of color.

"A freaking cockroach!" Tyler shouted. "It's the size of a school bus!"

The insect unfolded its spindly legs and scuttled up onto the field, testing the air with its antennae. Opal stared at its clicking, dripping jaws. She lifted the dagger, but her whole body quivered as she backed away. "Maybe . . . maybe we let this one disappear on its own."

The cockroach swung a feeler at Logan. He ducked the oozing appendage and darted toward the ATVs. "Time to go!" he shouted.

"Nico, let's bail!" Tyler wiped his slick forehead. "I'm not getting eaten by a bug, man. That's just wrong."

"No argument here," Nico said. The three boys converged

on the ATVs and took cover behind them. Opal edged their way, waving the dagger. It felt like threatening an elephant with a toothpick.

Emma hadn't moved. "This is my fault," she breathed. The cockroach swiveled its massive bulk, slapping a feeler in her direction. She dodged just in time, then ran for the others. The insect chittered in their direction.

"Is this one yours, Emma?" Nico whispered as they huddled behind the vehicles.

Emma nodded robotically. "*Roach Motel*. The one horror movie I could never finish."

Opal swallowed, eyes glued to the monster. Its antennae were probing the air again. "Why couldn't you finish?"

"*Why?!*" Tyler's voice cracked. "It's a giant cockroach! Plus the movie one had *poisonous fangs*."

"I'm out of here." Logan reached over and started his engine. "Who's coming with me?"

The figment's head snapped to them. With a grating, grinding hiss, it charged. Everyone scattered, Logan jumping out of the driver's seat just before the roach smashed into the purring vehicle. The monster flipped the four-wheeler upside down and sunk in its jaws.

Opal sprinted a short way, then stopped to catch her breath. The others joined her in a ragged knot.

"It's too fast!" Tyler wailed. "We can't outrun it, and the engine made it mad." The figment had turned on the other ATV, flipping it on its back as well.

"I'm so sorry, guys." Emma spoke in a thin, trembling voice. "When I was little I played baseball all the time. One day I went into the garage to get my glove. When I put my hand inside"—she shivered from head to toe—"three roaches crawled out. They ran up my arm and neck. Into my hair. One touched my *mouth*. *Roach Motel* was too much. Regular cockroaches are awful enough."

Opal wrapped an arm around her, shooting a glance at Nico. *What should we do?*

Nico shook his head. "I told the Sasquatch I was sorry."

"Forget that," Tyler growled. "Emma doesn't owe that thing an apology."

The giant roach lost interest in the vehicles. It swiveled to face the group, feelers dancing in the air.

The cockroach clicked, rearing up. Something lifted from its back.

"I forgot to tell you," Emma whispered in despair. "The movie monster can fly."

The cockroach rose like a storm cloud, blocking out the sun.

Opal lifted the dagger. But before she could do anything, Emma snatched it away and charged toward the figment. "Emma, no!" Nico shouted.

"Stop!" Tyler screamed, as Emma ran directly beneath the hovering figment.

"Fight it, Emma!" Opal yelled in desperation.

The cockroach plummeted from the sky, mandibles

clicking. Emma ducked under its jaws and slammed the dagger into its belly.

Opal heard a crunch, followed by a horrible *squish*. The roach collapsed with a rattling moan, its feelers swinging wildly. Emma scrambled out from between the insect's massive, flailing legs, covered in yellow bug guts but still holding the dagger. "That was *my* baseball glove!" she yelled.

She pulled the knife back to strike again.

Before she could, the figment vanished with a popping sound.

Opal nearly collapsed in surprise. Emma dropped the dagger and closed her eyes. Everyone reached her at once, smothering her in their arms.

"Are you hurt?" Opal ran her hands over Emma, hunting for a bite, a wound, a break.

"It didn't get me." Emma's whole body quaked. "That was close, though."

"Why'd you attack?" Tyler squawked. "These things are dangerous now!"

Emma looked to where the figment had been. "In the movie, right before I quit watching, the roach flew up high and a million tiny roaches exploded from it." She looked like she might puke. "I did *not* want that to happen."

"Wait." Logan held up a hand. "Did you kill the figment by stabbing it?"

"I don't know." Emma eyed the goo-covered dagger on the grass. "Maybe the knife has some kind of power. When it touched the figment, I felt something inside me let go. And we know it's connected to the island."

Logan frowned. "But Nico didn't have it when he beat the Sasquatch."

Nico held up his hands. "I'm not sure what I did. Or if I did anything at all."

Tyler's brow furrowed. "So how *do* we get rid of the figments?"

No one answered. A cold wind swept the clifftop, chilling Opal's bones.

"This isn't even close to fun anymore," Tyler said. "That mega-roach was Emma's biggest fear in the world. Why would the Darkdeep send that?" He frowned at the fog-shrouded path. "What else is waiting down there?"

Only the Darkdeep knows, Opal thought. *Our worst fears come to life.*

"Let's go home," she said. "Regroup. We don't have to go down into Still Cove today."

Fear lingered in Emma's eyes, in the set of her mouth. But she picked up the dagger and wiped it clean on the grass. Everyone stared at the strange weapon in her hand. Was it the answer?

"No," Emma said, gripping the knife firmly. "We do it now. Let's end this while we still can."

Without waiting for a response, she turned and strode for the trail.

29

NICO

Nico moved cautiously down the cliff-side path.

He couldn't see far in the cloying fog, which covered them like a damp towel. *What else is hiding in this?*

The others piled up behind him. "Are we really going inside the tunnel?" Tyler asked. "Not knowing what's down there?"

"No choice," Opal said. "That's where the floor carving is."

Tyler grunted in displeasure.

They passed the lone owl's nest like so many times before. But the bird was absent. Driven away by unnatural monsters? Nico hoped not.

The cave was blessedly empty. After a minute of careful surveillance—ears straining to detect any lurkers—Nico activated his phone light. Afraid to lose his nerve, he went straight for the tunnel. At the bottom of the switchbacks he led the group along the passage under the cove to the open chamber.

Everyone let out a relieved breath, but this was as far as their plan extended.

"So . . ." Tyler brushed at his nose. "Now what?"

Nico shrugged. "Any ideas?"

"Search the room." Opal held the dagger in her phone light. The hand-and-torch symbol gleamed on its odd hilt. "We're looking for anything like this. Maybe there's a hiding place."

"Or a Darkdeep off-switch." Logan began running his beam along the chamber walls. The others split up and did the same, but after five minutes they were back where they started.

"We're missing something," Tyler said. "Something obvious, I bet."

"Unless it's just a dumb carving," Emma mumbled. "Maybe Hale was into chiseling."

Nico took a knee on the floor. "The torch symbol brought us here, so maybe the carving itself matters. Can I get some more light?" The others clustered above him as Nico ran a hand along the weathered stone creases. His finger paused where the hand and torch met. He scratched at the dirt.

A black oval appeared.

"Oh, man!" Emma did a little dance step. "You found it, Nico!"

"I didn't find anything yet." But he wiggled his fingers at Opal excitedly. She handed him the dagger.

Nico slid the hilt into the oval-shaped gap. It fit perfectly, rotating with an easy click. Behind them, a section of wall dropped open. Sour air oozed from beyond.

"You gotta be kidding me." Tyler gripped his head. "Another secret room?"

Nico flew to the doorway. Beyond was a dark chamber of roughly the same size. The air was stale and tinged with flavors of decay. The walls and floor glowed with strange, sea-green spots. Shining his light, Nico spotted a stack of unlit torches on the ground. An old Zippo lighter rested in a nook above them.

Logan glanced around in confusion. "What's that glow?"

Nico lifted a torch from the pile. It was covered in a thick layer of mold and grime. He stripped off the foulness as best he could, then flipped open the lighter. The first few spins did nothing, but finally the wheel shot a spark.

Nico ignited the torch and passed it to Opal, then lifted another. Only the top few were salvageable—the rest had dissolved into mounds of slimy black mold. But Nico stuck with it and got three more blazing. Spotting brackets, Opal began setting the torches in the wall. They cast an eerie half-light over the room, creating a spectral feel.

Nico rose. He was desperately curious about who built this place. Who would construct a secret underground room? *Someone who wanted to hide something. To protect something.*

The room was circular, with grimy rectangles of sailcloth affixed to the wall: black-and-yellow checkerboard, a red diamond, a wide blue cross. Four wooden chests were positioned at the cardinal direction points. A heavy table occupied the center, set with half-melted candles. A pile of rotten papers sat in the middle.

"Those are signal flags." Emma pointed to the faded canvas emblems on the wall. "Nautical ones. The kind used by old ships to communicate at sea."

But yellow-green stains covered everything, coating large sections of the table and floor. Nico bent to examine one, then straightened quickly in disgust. "Slugs. Gross." He looked around. "Oh man, they're everywhere. That's why the room is glowing." Normally he'd be totally freaked out, but after a giant poisonous cockroach, regular slugs seemed manageable.

"Huh?" Logan said. "Because of slugs?"

"Bioluminescence," Opal explained. "These slugs make their own light. They must've gotten in here since Roman Hale died." She touched a finger to the slime. "Ugh. It's like glue."

Tyler waved at the rotten documents on the table. "Whatever this was . . . it's ruined."

Opal moved to one of the chests and pried at the lid. Its hinges groaned but eventually gave way. "Old books," she reported with a frown. "But the slugs got in here, too."

Logan and Emma opened two more chests and found the same. Tyler popped the last one. "Whoa. Check *this* out." He lifted a slime-covered dagger. "Just like from the warehouse, only no fancy key-hilt." He rummaged around inside. "There's a bunch of these bad boys in here."

Emma grabbed one and raised it in triumph. "This is the answer, you guys! We can fight the figments!"

Tyler began passing daggers out. Logan tried to spin one in his hand, but it clattered to the floor. He swept it back up with a sheepish grin. "No more running, Holland. Imaginary creatures beware!"

"For sure." But Nico wondered. He knew he should've been pumped—Emma had to be right—but something about magical weapons rang false to him. He hadn't had a special figment-killing dagger when facing the Sasquatch. *Maybe I just got lucky there.*

Nico set down his knife and approached the table, taking care where he stepped. The same motto from Roman Hale's stone cylinder was etched into its surface: *ACCIPERE VIC-TUS.* The mold seemed to be growing from a single large book. Nico could barely read the spine.

Index of Torchbearers: 1741—

"You guys, come over here."

Opal looked up, must've seen something in his eyes. She hurried to join him. The others did the same. Nico pointed to the slimy, dilapidated book. "I think this was a list of people who watched over the Darkdeep in the past."

Logan frowned. "Why do you say that?"

231

Nico pointed to the title. "This sounds like a roster."

"Open it, Nico," Tyler said. He made no move to touch the slug-strewn pages himself.

Nose wrinkling, Nico carefully flipped the moldy cover. Half of it fell apart in his fingers. What remained of the first page was a column of names and dates, the oldest entries smudged and fading. Some entries were in elegant script, others crudely scribbled and barely legible. The most recent looked like it had been written in blue ballpoint pen.

"Torchbearer 115." Emma pointed to the bottom entry. "Roman Hale."

"The last name in the book," Opal said quietly. "And look at the signature above his. Clarisse Barquera. It looks way older than Roman's. I think he was the only Torchbearer for a long time."

Nico felt his heart squeeze. "The guy probably had an accident. Or maybe a heart attack. He fell into that ravine and died, and there wasn't another Torchbearer to take his place."

"No one was guarding the Darkdeep," Tyler whispered. "Then we showed up."

Opal nodded grimly. "That's why the houseboat was empty, and why this room is such a mess. There hasn't been a caretaker."

Logan huffed a frustrated sigh. "This is important, but it doesn't help us. We still don't know how to stop the Darkdeep now that it's gone crazy."

"Not true." Emma's jaw firmed in a determined line. "We have daggers now. Figments can't stand against us. We can regain control of the island."

Nico met Opal's eye, saw his uneasiness mirrored there. "You think that's it?" he asked.

"I'm not sure." She chewed her bottom lip. "Could be. You saw what happened when Emma used one." Nico gave a hesitant nod. Could it be that easy?

"That book has more pages," Logan prodded. "Maybe we should read them?"

Nico shook free of his troubled thoughts. He turned the page, most of it disintegrating in his hand, but he could read the next chapter title. A whistle escaped his lips.

" 'Nature of the Deep,' " Opal blurted. "Jackpot!"

Nico stared at the slug-smeared words. This book might contain all the answers they'd been searching for, but it was literally falling to pieces.

Tyler nodded at the phrase carved into the table. "*Accept to Overcome*. I wonder what that's about."

The others stared at him in shock. It took Tyler a moment to notice. "What? What'd I do? It's Latin."

Emma shoved him with both hands. "Get out. You know Latin?"

"My dad studied it in college," Tyler said defensively. "He made me learn some. I'm not great at it or anything." Nico tried to flip forward in the book, but the next few pages were stuck together. Part of the binding came free in his hands. "Stupid slime."

"It's completely ruined." Opal covered her face.

Nico kept leafing the crumbling pages. "This says something about . . . reading the spirit. Look, here." He tapped a series of faded lines. "The Deepness . . . it *projects*. Or maybe the word is *infects*. Which, of course, is totally different." He squeezed his eyes shut in frustration. A slug edged onto his hand and he flung it away with a yelp.

Tyler patted his shoulder. "Keep trying. Maybe we can dig something out of this mess."

Nico sighed all the way down to his shoes, but he kept digging through the book, hunting for anything legible. Logan made as if to speak, but Nico shushed him. Finally, he found a clearer section of text. Everyone leaned in so they could read at the same time.

Tyler spoke first. "Well, that doesn't sound good."

"I think it's saying the Darkdeep reads minds." Opal tapped the page with her fingernail. "Listen: *The Deepness explores the psyche and latches on, pulling an impression into being.*"

"What's the Deepness?" Logan asked.

"The Darkdeep." Emma waved a dismissive hand. "Our name is better."

Nico ignored them both, focusing on Opal. "But we knew that. The figments come from our imaginations."

"I think it's more," she said. "I think this means the Dark-deep gets *into* you somehow, once you enter the pool. Here's the next line: *Subjects carry the Deepness beyond the vortex in a symbiosis that can, if unchecked, become parasitic.*"

Tyler's faced soured. "I do not like that sentence."

"Nope," Logan agreed.

"What if you stop doing it?" Emma asked nervously. "And don't go in anymore?"

Tyler shook his head. "Not sure. But it's saying figments spring from people, not the pool. The water is just the Dark-deep's cage."

"Cage?" Nico's skin prickled.

Tyler crossed his arms peevishly. "I *think* that's what it says, but the ink's all run together and there's slug juice every-where." He shivered. "If the Darkdeep stays inside you, that might explain why figments don't show up on film. They're projected from within."

"What about the daggers?" Emma asked. "Any mention of them?"

"Not that I can make out," Tyler grumbled. Opal shook her head.

"I don't see anything about shutting it down, either," Nico added glumly.

"This part is the worst." Opal pointed to the bottom of the page. "*Once engaged, the cycle grows stronger over time. The Deepness can escape if it isn't Watched.* The last word is capitalized. I bet this is talking about Torchbearers. They must do something to contain the Darkdeep."

Nico felt a cold sweat dampen his temples. "What happens if it escapes?"

"Nothing good." Opal tapped the bottommost paragraph. "*Above all else, one must never let the Deepness feed on fears. It will strengthen and hunger, becoming more powerful with each mind it touches.*" Her voice broke as she stepped back from the last line. "Guys, we have to stop this thing before it reaches more people. Or else . . ."

Silence.

Logan finally broke it. "Or what?"

Opal stared at him with glistening eyes.

"It breaks free," she whispered. "And can never be sealed again."

30
OPAL

Opal led the group from the tunnel.

The island was deathly quiet, as though it were holding its breath. "Looks clear," Nico whispered, scanning the gully. "Let's hurry. I don't want another fight if we can help it."

Everyone carried a Torchbearer dagger. They were headed for the pool.

"Time to finish this," Opal said. How? She didn't know. But they had to face the Darkdeep and stop it.

She started up the ridge. At its crest, she paused. Opal couldn't see the houseboat through the fog, but the pond was rippling oddly, as if deep waves moved under its surface. *Just keep moving.*

They climbed down to the field, sticking close together. But as they neared the water it heaved upward, surging in a powerful wave. A monstrous black head rose from the surface.

Logan froze, eyes popping. "What is *that* thing?!"

"Figment! Run!" Nico pointed to the stepping-stones. "Get to the houseboat!"

Opal's sneakers kicked up dirt as she ran. Emma was beside her, clutching her dagger. Logan, Nico, and Tyler fanned out as the group pounded across the grass.

"It's the Beast!" Tyler shrieked, naked panic in his voice. "It's real, I knew it!"

Opal's stomach lurched. She risked a glance at the pond and wished she hadn't.

Mouth and teeth and pain.

The creature was enormous, its maw filled with razor-sharp teeth. It had the sleek body of a sea serpent—a mountain of writhing indigo—but it clawed out of the water on thick muscular legs. Scales glimmered along the Beast's entire length, and its eyes were black puddles of oil.

The creature's wail shook the earth. Then it *moved,* faster than a blink, tearing across the grass to plant itself in their path. Logan slid to a stop as the monster's jaws snapped an inch from his head. He bolted back to where the others huddled in terror.

"Get out your weapons!" Emma yelled. "It's our only chance!"

Tyler grabbed her by the arm. "Forget the stupid daggers, we have to go! *The Beast is here.* I knew it was real!" He was on the verge of a total meltdown.

Opal understood. His worst nightmare was stalking toward them, gnashing its teeth.

"Tyler, listen!" Opal said. "That's a figment, not the Beast. It isn't real!"

The Beast roared and charged, gouging the earth with its clawed feet. Tyler collapsed into a ball and covered his head. Emma lunged sideways, her dagger tumbling to the grass. The monster followed her movement, jaws chomping the empty air where she'd stood a moment before.

Opal spun the other way, fleeing blindly. Without another option, she dove into the pond.

The icy water nearly stopped Opal's heart. She kicked beneath the surface as a frustrated roar echoed into the depths. When she ran out of breath, Opal spluttered to the surface, wiping liquid from her eyes.

Logan and Nico ran to help Emma. The Beast thrashed around on the field, trying to snatch Nico in its teeth. Logan went down, clutching his knee. Emma was shouting in Tyler's ear, trying to drag him toward the woods, but he seemed unable to move.

As Opal watched, Nico threw himself behind a downed tree and wriggled under it. The Beast twisted away, spotting Emma and Tyler. It stormed at them, roaring in fury. "Look out!" Opal screamed.

Tyler scrambled to his feet. He pushed Emma behind him and lifted his dagger. The Beast slowed to a stalking pace, its black eyes gleaming. Tyler squared his shoulders.

The creature halted. Saliva dripped from its mouth as it regarded Tyler curiously. Seconds ticked past as the two locked eyes, one rumbling like a dragon, the other shaking like a leaf.

The Beast snarled. Its head darted forward in a deadly strike.

Tyler sprang, sidestepping the Beast and stabbing it in the neck. Black blood spurted from the wound. The Beast reared back and howled, ripping the dagger from Tyler's fingers.

But the figment didn't vanish.

"No," Opal breathed, dripping in the shallow water.

"It didn't work!" Tyler backed away, his voice cracking as he stared up at the supernatural predator. "Everyone get out of here! I'll . . . I'll . . ."

Nico and Logan were crouching at the edge of the woods—too far away to reach Tyler before the Beast struck again—but Emma shot forward to stand beside him, clutching her dagger.

The Beast's eyes shifted to her.

"Emma, *get back*," Tyler ordered, his voice raw with fear. Quick as a rumor, the Beast swung its tail, smacking Tyler in the chest and knocking him down. In the next second it wheeled on Emma.

"Run!" Opal screamed.

The Beast whipped its tail again, sweeping Emma's feet. The dagger bounced from her fingers. The monster dipped its face close to hers and seemed to smile, baring an acre of jagged teeth as it prepared to finish its kill.

"Emma!"

Tyler scooped up her dagger and threw it as hard as he could. The blade punched into the Beast's side.

Its eyes widened. A howl of pain shook the island.

The Beast shimmered and disappeared.

"Holy crap." Opal waded out of the water as Nico and Logan emerged from the trees. Opal picked up the key dagger from where she'd dropped it on the grass.

Tyler and Emma were slumped side by side, chests heaving. They gave each other a shaky fist bump.

"Let's get out of here," Logan said, his voice sharp.

Nico put a hand on Tyler's shoulder. "You okay, man?"

"Fine," Tyler wheezed. "Never better. Bring on more Beasts."

"I don't get it." Opal was staring at the weapon in her hand. "The dagger didn't work, but then it did?"

"No idea," Tyler said weakly. "Seriously. I just saw it go after Emma and reacted."

A biting wind swept the island, chilling Opal's skin. She felt a sudden sense of impending loss. "We should get inside," she said. "Right now."

But before anyone could move, a black-robed figure emerged from the woods. The creature carried a scythe. Its robe didn't ripple in the wind.

Opal knew exactly who it was. *My turn.*

"All of you need to go," she said in a shaky voice. "Get to the houseboat."

Nico shook his head, staring at the dark apparition. "No way, Opal. What is that?"

"It's Death." Opal gripped the key dagger tightly. "This one came from me. I'll follow after . . ."

"Opal, that's *Death*." Emma swallowed. "No one can fight Death."

Opal laughed a little wildly. "I sure hope you're wrong."

The specter slid smoothly across the grass. Stalks in its path crinkled and died.

Opal took a deep breath. "I just have to conquer my fear. That's how you guys did it."

"I don't thi—" Nico began, but she cut him off.

"You're wasting time. *Please*. This one is mine."

Death halted ten yards away. Opal's breath began to mist.

"You have to stop the Darkdeep," Opal whispered. "We need to *end this*. Now go."

Death lofted its gleaming scythe. Logan turned and sprinted for the stepping-stones.

"Be strong," Tyler whispered. "It's only a figment, not the Reaper." He grabbed Emma's hand. "Come on."

Tears spilled onto Emma's cheeks. Her gaze flicked to Opal, who nodded. Emma bit her lip, then turned and ran with Tyler.

Nico didn't budge.

"Nico, please. Finish the job. I've got this, but I need to do it alone."

Emotions warred on Nico's face. "You better be right behind me," he said roughly, echoing her from the night before. She heard him groan helplessly, but he spun and jogged away.

Opal released a shaky breath. *This is how you face Death. Alone.*

The Reaper moved forward again. Ice-white hands gripped the scythe's black handle.

Come and get me. Opal clutched the dagger so hard her fingers ached. *I'm not as defenseless as you think.* But her heart pounded. How could anyone face Death without fear?

She took a tiny step back. Then another.

Death closed in. *It always catches you in the end.*

The scythe's shadow fell across Opal's body. Terror pulsed through her veins. Her breath hitched, halted, hung in the air. Death pulled back its hood. Eyes of nothing stared down at her.

I am the end of everything.

Opal screamed. The sound echoed through her, awakening her blood, her bones.

She ran from Death as fast as she could.

31

NICO

The Darkdeep seethed like a hurricane.

Nico stared into the convulsing blackness as eerie lights strobed on the walls.

This was it. There was nothing between them and the whirlpool.

"Hurry, Nico!" Emma pointed to the dagger in his hand.

"Throw it in!" Tyler cringed behind them while Logan kept an eye on the staircase. Where was Opal?

Nico hefted the blade. Was that the answer? Could he stop the Darkdeep by attacking it somehow? His instincts rebelled against such a simple solution—*how could a dagger hurt a swirling pool of water?*—but he didn't know what else to do.

The houseboat trembled with the force of the Darkdeep's spin. Nico worried the planking might come apart. He worried *everything* was coming apart.

There was a crash upstairs, then Opal came racing down the steps. Ignoring everyone, she slumped down against the far wall and hugged her knees to her chest.

"Opal?" Nico called. She didn't respond, eyes wide with panic. The encounter with Death must've shaken her badly. *You think, Nico? Who wouldn't be messed up about that?*

But Nico couldn't help her now. His gut told him time was running out. The Darkdeep sloshed and boiled, a tempest rampaging out of control. He stepped to the edge, palms sweating. *How do you stop a force of nature?*

Nico raised the knife and was about to throw it into the well when a dark form emerged from the shadows across the room.

His heart nearly stopped. Something was in there with them. Before he could yell out a warning, it stepped into the ghostly light.

All the blood in Nico's body rushed to his head, then plunged through the floor.

He couldn't breathe. He was staring at the impossible.

He was looking at his father.

Warren Holland stomped around the pool, glaring at Nico from his intimidating height. "Nico, what do you think you're doing?"

Nico gaped, unable to respond. What was his *dad* doing here? How did he find the houseboat? How did he get to the island?

Warren crossed his arms. "Nico, I'm incredibly disap-pointed. Do you have any idea how embarrassing this is for me? This little stunt of yours could cost me my job!"

"We . . . I didn't . . ." Nico stammered. "I wasn't trying . . . I . . . I fell . . ."

Warren shook his head, his voice thick with disgust. "You didn't *think* is what happened. Like always. I work my fingers to the bone every day to take care of you and your brother, and here you are causing trouble behind my back. I've had it with you! You can't do anything right."

Tears burned in Nico's eyes. "I'm sorry, Dad. I didn't mean—"

Someone took his hand. Nico recoiled in alarm, but the fingers held tight.

Opal. She was up off the floor and standing by his side.

"You've done nothing but screw up lately," Warren Hol-land continued, his voice heated. "That's why I'm never around. I don't *want* to see you. I don't *want* to be in that house."

Something cold seized Nico's chest, like he was already drowning inside the Darkdeep's black current.

He's telling the truth. He doesn't love me.

"Nico, I'm right here," Opal said firmly. "Don't listen to this monster. It's not real."

Nico blinked. His knees began to shake.

Opal was watching Warren Holland like a hawk. "Nico, look at his eyes."

Almost against his will, Nico met his father's glare. He saw nothing but loathing there. "You're a failure, boy." Warren nodded as if making a proclamation. "I wish you weren't my son."

Opal squeezed Nico's hand, anchoring him. "No! Look again. Nico, look *hard*."

Nico's legs wobbled, but he didn't fall. Someone was at his back, standing firm. He turned to find Tyler there, with Emma beside him. She put a hand on Nico's shoulder. Even Logan joined the group, glowering at Nico's father, who continued scowling at them all like they'd stolen something.

"It's not real," Opal repeated. "We're with you."

Nico sucked in a shaky breath. Met his father's piercing stare. The anger was still there, but also . . . something else. The whites of his father's eyes. They were . . . glowing. They were red.

"He's a figment," Opal whispered. "This isn't your father. It's your fear."

Warren moved closer to the churning, thrashing pool. "My job is all that matters, Nico. I don't care how it affects you. That's not important. It was never important."

"Don't listen," Tyler hissed. "That isn't your father, it's a monster. It's *your* monster, Nico. You can handle it. We've got your back."

Nico gasped, his head spinning like the frigid pool. "But . . . it might . . . some of it . . ."

"Doesn't matter." Opal pointed at Warren Holland. "That is a nightmare, and it needs to go away now."

His father's voice filled with menace. "Nico, get away from those brats. They aren't your friends. They're using you. They're *laughing* at you."

"That's a bunch of crap!" Emma darted forward and jabbed her finger in Warren's face. "Say whatever you want, *liar*, but he's got us. We'll always have his back."

Warren's red-tinged eyes narrowed. His hands curled into fists.

Nico slid in front of Emma and went nose to nose with his father. "You're not real." He wiped his eyes. Nico's fear morphed to anger and he let it run. "What you said isn't true. But even if it is, I'll be fine. I have people who care about me. I'm not alone."

The figment of Warren Holland glared at Nico, a vein throbbing in its neck. When it made no further move, Nico put a hand to his father's uniformed chest. "Get out of here."

He pushed.

His fingers shot through to nothing as Warren Holland vanished.

Nico felt something lift from his spirit. He took a rasping, choking inhale as Opal, Tyler, and Emma swarmed him in a hug. Logan stood a foot away and gave Nico an awkward shoulder pat.

The Darkdeep exploded.

A column of black liquid shot up from the pool to

hammer against the ceiling, showering the room with icy droplets. At the same time, something metal scraped against the staircase.

Tyler ran over and looked up. "The Reaper's back!" His voice shook with fear. Opal broke toward the steps.

Nico wanted to help her, like she had him, but couldn't tear his eyes from the Darkdeep. Inside it, something dark took form. The ghostly outline of a face appeared. It stared at Nico with hollow eyes.

Despair flooded Nico's mind. He wanted to whimper in fear but was too terrified to make a sound. He knew instinctively that this was no figment.

This was the Darkdeep.

It had come to finish them.

"Oh man, we're so screwed," Tyler whispered. Freezing black rain continued to fall around them. Emma and Logan backed against the wall.

Nico heard Death's scythe hit the basement floor, trapping them in the chamber.

Opal planted herself before the Reaper.

"I get it now," she said in a shaky voice. "It's not enough to face you. I have to accept you, too." She lifted Roman Hale's dagger. "*Accept to Overcome*. I have to accept my fear, because *it's* real, even if you're not."

The Reaper raised its scythe. Brought it crashing to the floorboards.

I am the end of everything.

249

Opal cringed, almost fled. But this time she stood tall.

"No," she whispered. "You're not." Her voice slowly gained strength. "I'll die one day, but that's okay. Everyone does. I still have today. I have my friends. I'm not alone."

The Reaper pulled back its scythe, but Opal was quicker. She stepped close and gently brushed its sleeve.

The moment she made contact, Death disappeared. Opal shuddered once, then smiled.

A shriek thundered from the Darkdeep. The column of black water expanded, doubling in size. The wraithlike face reappeared and pushed against the surface. Nico saw the outline of huge hands. The water bulged outward, taking shape.

"It's trying to come out!" Emma cried. "Run!"

"No!" Nico shouted. This *had* to stop. It *had* to end.

"Fear, Nico!" Opal darted to his side. "The Darkdeep feeds on fear! We can't let it win."

Nico realized he was still holding his dagger. He flung it into the water column, but the knife passed straight through and bounced off the far wall. The creature seeped forward, revealing a humanlike form, except for its ghastly head and gigantic hands. It was nearly out, rounding into a liquid nightmare above the well.

Nico thought furiously. He had to find some way to fight it.

The Darkdeep feeds off fear.

Fear. Inside us.

The creature stepped over the lip of the pool, a wicked snarl curling its lips.

Fear connects us. Binds us.

I'm bound to the Darkdeep.

Nico's eyes popped. He met the creature's empty gaze.

I have to sever the binding.

Nico grabbed Opal's hand. "Are you with me?"

She stared at him for a moment, then her eyes widened.

Nico squeezed. Opal squeezed back.

"Yes," she whispered.

A heart-stopping scream split the air.

Together they faced the Darkdeep as it fought to escape the water.

Together, they dove in.

———————

Dark.

Wet.

Cold.

Nico floated in space, paralyzed by dread.

Darkness was all around him. Suffocating him. Stealing his spirit in tiny, greedy bites.

The Darkdeep slunk from the black. It reached for Nico's throat, but something jerked him away.

A hand.

I have hands, and someone is holding mine.

Opal. He thought of her, and she appeared beside him. The water was everywhere, but also nowhere, as if they drifted in a void. *Are we still in the pond? Is this a real place?*

The creature regarded them with unmistakable malice. Figments appeared in the void.

The cockroach. The Beast. Death and its scythe.

Nico's fingers tightened around Opal's. He remembered them riding bikes, inventing new worlds. It made him stronger. More grounded in whatever emptiness they occupied. They faced the nightmares together.

We don't fear you. Opal thought rather than spoke. *Not anymore.*

This ends now. Nico closed his eyes, concentrating. *It's time for the figments to go.*

One by one, the imaginary creatures winked out. The Darkdeep howled.

Nico felt a sliver of hope, like a window opening to let in fresh air.

You don't belong here. Opal pointed at the Darkdeep. *This isn't your place.*

It screamed. The creature stretched larger, its face a mask of naked fury.

Chains, Opal thought. Clinking iron links materialized around the Darkdeep's wrists. It bellowed in rage, fighting to get free. But Opal had solved the riddle. Nico knew what to do.

Dagger, Nico thought, and a weapon appeared in his hand.

The Darkdeep's roar now carried a note of fear. Opal held a dagger, too.

Go, Opal sent. *Or we'll finish you.*

The Darkdeep squealed like a cornered weasel. As Nico watched it attack the chains, he spied a thrumming black line shooting from its back. The cord was both there and not there, extending high overhead.

Nico looked up. Saw the bottom of the houseboat.

The connection to our world.

Nico zoomed close to the monster. Opal appeared next to him instantly.

The Darkdeep's hollow eyes widened. Its mouth opened.

Nico and Opal thought as one.

Time to go.

Two daggers sliced through the pulsing black cord.

The line snapped.

The Darkdeep wailed as it was sucked backward into the endless void.

Black flipped to white. Up became down.

Nico's eyes rolled up and he remembered nothing more.

32

OPAL

Y ou look amazing."

Opal was hiding a grin.

"Shut up." Nico blushed the color of his radish outfit. He couldn't sit properly because the body was too round, so he lolled uncomfortably to one side. A lounging vegetable. "Why couldn't I just show you a photo of the costume or something?"

"We needed to see it in person," Tyler said. "Definitely. Couldn't get the full effect otherwise."

"Wait till you see Opal's dance," Emma said.

Opal shook her head ruefully. "I thought you had my back."

"I do." Emma schooled her face to absolute seriousness. "Your routine is a masterpiece."

"I'm excited to watch the movie," Opal said. "And to see how many radishes Tyler can eat."

"Which reminds me—I brought a radish pie." Tyler placed it on the showroom floor, in the middle of their lopsided circle. "It's actually supposed to taste good. I think there's a whole bag of sugar in it."

Nico made another attempt to get upright. "Why am I wearing this nightmare again?"

"We need a ceremony to formally make us Torchbearers, but I didn't want some creepy ancient ritual." Tyler set a bowl of raw radishes next to the pie. "No robes, no chanting or dagger kissing, no group haircuts. I've had enough weird for a while."

"Well I hope ridiculous is okay." Opal adjusted the cuffs on her outfit—a red tracksuit covered in glitter glue. They'd agreed to perform their individual festival obligations as part of the ceremony, since none of them actually got to participate. They'd all been grounded for going missing after town square got trashed.

Nico grinned. "I can't believe my dad thought that not being a radish was punishment."

Opal grinned back at him. There was still no official word on whether Nico's father was getting transferred, but Nico wasn't letting that get him down. Opal knew he was determined to enjoy every moment he had in Timbers. She said another silent prayer that the Hollands stayed put.

"It was punishment for me," Emma grumbled. "I was ready to slay that movie."

Opal snorted. "So now we're punishing ourselves."

Tyler was staring at the radish bowl. "Can't believe I'm going to eat these things."

"I wish Logan had come," Emma said. They all went quiet.

Logan had been distant since the Darkdeep battle, after Opal and Nico were spit out into the pond. It seemed like he wanted to forget the whole thing. Opal was disappointed, but not totally surprised. At least he didn't hassle Nico anymore. *He said he was sorry. That's something.*

"You did invite him, right?" Tyler asked Opal.

"Yeah." Opal shrugged. "He wasn't a jerk about it or anything. But he said he had something else to do." It wouldn't be riding his four-wheelers. Those had been mangled by a giant cockroach.

Nico glanced at his watch. "Let's get started. If I come home late again, I'm toast."

"Right. Okay." Tyler cleared his throat. "And thus we begin our sacred ceremony on this hallowed Saturday afternoon."

Nico rolled his eyes. "Can I take this stupid costume off yet?"

"You have to *parade* first," Emma scolded. "And wear the hat, please."

"*Gah.* Help me up, then." Nico held out his arms like a baby. Laughing, the girls hoisted him to his feet. He strutted back and forth along the center aisle. "I'm a little radish, walking down the street. Got a stem on my head and roots for my feet." He tried to do a spin but toppled over. Everyone cracked up, including Nico.

Opal laughed with the others, but something tugged at her. She glanced at the smashed wall panel, courtesy of three deadly orc figments. They'd hung a sheet across the opening, but Opal knew that a dark pool lurked underneath them, its black surface still as glass.

For now.

"You next, Ty." Nico removed his radish cap and swatted his friend with it. "Let's see how many you can eat."

Emma pulled up her phone timer. "Three minutes to glory. Go!"

"I'm not going to survive this." Tyler picked up a radish and popped it into his mouth. He made a gagging face. "*Ack. Blech.* Help me, I'm dying." It turned out he could only eat two.

"And you thought you'd win." Nico wagged his head in mock disgust.

"These things are rough." Tyler spat into a plastic bag. "The pie better be good."

"Okay, Opal, you're up," Nico said. They'd already decided Emma's movie would be last. They'd watch together and cheer for the killer radish-tomatoes.

Opal rose primly to her feet. "I need you all to be respectful. This is art. I am an artist."

Emma began playing soft classical music on her phone.

Opal wilted to the floor. "I am a seed. A tiny seed, full of radish potential."

Tyler snorted. "Are you seriously going to narrate?"

"*Shhh*. Listen carefully." Opal lofted an arm. "I am a seed, *growing*." It was a struggle to keep a straight face. "Soon, I shall emerge from the earth." She popped to her feet in a toe-point.

"That was fast," Nico cracked.

"I'm not done," Opal admonished. "I'm *still* emerging." She stretched her arms up high, then yanked them down to her sides and started doing the running man.

"Killing it," Emma said appreciatively.

"For the finale, you all must emerge with me." Opal beckoned them up off the floor.

Tyler groaned, but Emma switched the music to a pop song. Opal hoisted Nico to his feet and he started doing an awkward radish-robot move. They were all dancing like fools when they heard the front door open.

Everyone froze, eyes widening.

Logan Nantes walked into the room.

The group gasped in relief. Opal felt her cheeks flame. They were acting like dorks and she was wearing a homemade vegetable outfit. This was the exact kind of thing bullies crushed people for.

"So." Logan's voice was awkward. "Is this, like, a radish . . . dance party?"

"Yes," Opal said. "It, uh . . . yes. Yes it is." The music played on.

To Opal's surprise, Logan dropped to the carpet and started doing the worm.

Everyone stared.

"What?" Logan popped back up and shrugged. "Worms help radishes grow."

Nico snorted. He held out a fist, and Logan bumped it.

"That was the least cool thing I've ever seen," Tyler said. "I'm impressed."

Opal laughed, and Emma cranked the volume. Soon everyone was cutting up and bouncing to the beat.

When the song ended, Logan signaled for Emma to pause the music. "Sorry I'm late. I wanted to bring something, but it took longer than I thought to make these." He pulled five black cords from his pocket, each strung with a tiny, hand-carved wooden torch.

Opal glanced at the faces framed on the wall. It was the Torchbearers' symbol, made new.

"It's like you guys said." Logan cleared his throat, handing the necklaces out one by one. "We're Torchbearers now. We should look the part."

Opal rotated the carving in her hand. Held upside down, the blazing fire looked like a whirling well. *Beautiful*.

"Did you make these yourself?" Emma asked in astonishment.

"Yeah. I hope it counts as my festival entry. I hate radishes."

"Hey!" Tyler barked. "Radishes are hot right now. Get on board."

Emma put her necklace on. "Oh, this counts just fine. They're amazing."

"Thanks, man." Tyler wrapped his around his wrist like a bracelet.

Opal did the same.

"So what's next?" Logan asked. "Do we swear an oath or something?"

"We were going to listen to Emma butcher a classic movie." Opal arched an eyebrow. "But an oath sounds good." She put her hand out, and the others stacked theirs on top. Everyone inhaled, but no one said anything.

"Still got nothing," Tyler said.

"One for all, and all for one?" Emma suggested.

Logan squinted. "I think that's backward."

Nico spoke in a quiet voice. "How about: *We watch the Darkdeep, and watch out for each other*." When the others looked at him, he ducked his head. "Lame. Never mind."

"No." Opal smiled. "It's great, Nico. Super lame, but also kind of perfect."

They all said the words. Lifted their hands together.

"Okay," Emma announced. "Movie time!"

She started fiddling with the portable projector she'd

brought. The movie flickered to life on a wall panel near the smashed one. Opal shivered again. *We really have to fix that.*

Emma began her dramatic voiceover. Tyler and Logan started mocking the horrible special effects. Opal noticed Nico was sitting close enough for their shoulders to touch. Was it on purpose? She couldn't tell.

A glint of light caught her attention—the projector's beam reflecting off the weird green jar on its pedestal. Opal glanced at the creature inside. It stared back with vacant, open eyes. *So strange*, Opal thought. *I wonder what it was.*

The creature blinked.

Opal gasped.

The Thing in a Jar smiled.

Come, Opal.

Come and see what I have for you.